LET LOVE IN

A.D. ELLIS

ONE

JACOB "JAKE" OAKLEY

So, this was how I would die. A heart attack at age forty. Was a heart attack caused by your heart beating too fast? Or from stopping completely? Because mine was doing an odd combination of both.

I stood at the door—a door I instantly regretted softly tapping on and gently pushing open without an invitation—and watched as Keegan danced. I'd come to ask the younger man—the *much* younger man, as in almost two decades younger—if he wanted dinner.

I thought maybe he needed a break from homework. I thought maybe he needed a friend. What I hadn't thought was that I'd find Keegan, dancing in my spare room, in only silky blue panties trimmed with lace.

I must have gasped at what I saw because Keegan whipped around with a shocked look on his face.

God damn, man. Stop looking at him. But I couldn't look away from his pale, creamy skin. He wasn't muscle-bound, but his chest, abs, and arms had definition. Keegan had a long, lithe body and it had been moving perfectly as he danced. His ass cupped in the silky panties as he moved had almost been too much. But the bulge in the front nearly brought me to my knees.

With a mumbled apology, I backed away from the door and escaped the room with only a slight stumble. Since when had a nearly naked man, even one in silk panties, nearly done me in?

I retreated to the kitchen and took a deep breath. Homemade pizzas were on stone slabs in the oven and I popped open a locally brewed cider to drink while I chopped up a salad. I needed to regroup and figure out a few things.

First, what the hell had I just seen Keegan doing?

Duh, dumbass. Pretty sure it looked like he was dancing in his room in silk and lace panties.

I rolled my eyes and swigged the cider.

I hadn't known Keegan long. Correction, I'd known *of* him for quite a while. But I'd only met him in person within the last two days. Pinching the bridge of my nose, I let my scattered thoughts piece themselves together.

Keegan was the son of my best friend.

My best friend, Gary "Doc" Wilson hadn't known about Keegan until a few years ago. Doc—who looked exactly like the character from Back to the Future, hence the nickname —had always been flighty, free-spirited, and extremely ungrounded. He'd take off to the ends of the earth on the slightest of whims. To say he wasn't the most stable of parents was possibly the biggest understatement of the year.

So, when Keegan's mom passed away, Doc was thrilled to learn of his son. But within a few months of getting to know Keegan, Doc got that itch and started taking off on wild journeys while leaving his teen son with Doc's sister or a housekeeper.

A few years later, with twenty-two-year-old Keegan within a year of finishing his online degree in trauma informed care,

Doc opted to sell his house and move to some remote island halfway across the world.

"So, you're just leaving your son on his own?" I'd asked my best friend of over three decades. I'd never been married, didn't have kids, but even I could see that maybe this wasn't the most parent-like thing to do.

Doc had waved me off. "Keeg can come with me. I'd love it. If not, he can live with my sister."

I'd frowned. "Your sister now lives in one of the most crowded cities in the country." I knew from what Doc had told me that Keegan didn't do well in crowds and did best in peaceful, calm situations. "You're asking him to leave his home *or* move somewhere he'd likely be extremely uncomfortable. He's going to school, how's he going to support himself?"

Doc had grinned broadly, but I knew his mind was already on his future adventure. "My father left Keegan a large sum of money. Once he graduates, the money is his. He's taking courses online, he can do that from anywhere."

"Neither of those choices seem to be best for Keegan based on what you've told me of him." I was used to always trying to bring Doc down and make him think things through.

Doc had gotten a wild look in his eyes. "Jake, my man, you're so damn right. What was I thinking. You've got that big ol' house out in the middle of nowhere. Keegan could stay with you. You're my very best friend, no one I'd trust my son with more than you."

Even as a grown man, I had a hard time saying no to Doc. Would it be a hardship to let the kid—who Doc described as shy and quiet—stay in one of my spare rooms? I could let him finish his degree, get his feet under him, and inherit the money his grandfather left for him before pushing him out into the big, bad world.

"Only if Keegan knows he has other options, I don't want him thinking he's being forced to live here," I'd agreed. Although, between the three options, I had a feeling staying with me was likely the only one that wouldn't scare the living daylights out of the kid.

So, two days ago, Keegan had driven his vintage VW Bug —a gift from Doc before he left—up the long, winding lane to my house. The greetings had been awkward, but Keegan had been polite and appreciative.

The first two days and nights he'd been there had been strange. He'd stayed in his room, snuck to the kitchen only when he didn't think I was around, and never ventured to any other parts of the house.

And now I'd walked in on him during what was clearly a private time.

Dumbass. Barging into his room is probably the worst way in the world to make him feel welcome and comfortable.

I huffed and drained the rest of my cider. So, Keegan liked to dance and wear silk and lace. Okay. I could deal.

But I had to get a handle on things.

Keegan and I needed to sit down and get some ground rules set.

I wanted the kid to know he was welcome and safe in my home. I didn't want the next year or so to consist of him hiding in his room.

Why not? You hide in your studio most of the time.

Rolling my eyes—again—I popped open a second cider and tossed the veggies into the salad I'd just chopped. I had no doubt that Keegan definitely wouldn't be joining me for dinner, so I packaged up some of the pizza slices and put them in the front of the fridge so he'd be sure to find the leftovers when he ventured out late at night.

Okay, I'd give both of us some time to get over the embarrassment of me walking in on him. Then we'd sit down and build some house rules. Hopefully, after a bit of time, Keegan would feel comfortable being around me and not just stuck in his room.

After I'd finished my salad, pizza, and cider, I went to my studio and set to work on my newest carving. I worked for the local college writing curriculums and teaching online classes, but I also made hand-carved wood pieces and sold them online.

Money had never been a huge issue for me—thanks to my parents leaving me every cent they had—but I made decent money at the college and I made more than I ever thought I would make with my carvings.

I wasn't sure when I'd stopped enjoying being in crowds and out in public. But I definitely preferred to stay home and only be around one or two people at a time. Online curriculum writing and teaching was perfect for me. I only had to go into the college from time-to-time and wood carving kept me calm and sane.

An hour or so later, I put down the piece and stretched. I was done for the evening, but the earlier incident with Keegan was still weighing heavily on my mind. After getting a drink in the kitchen, I stood in the hallway for several moments. I could go to my room and face Keegan the next day. Or I could go set things straight before bed.

I knew I wouldn't sleep if I was worrying about Keegan.

I padded toward his door and knocked.

No answer.

I knocked again. "Keegan?"

A shuffling sounded behind the door and then a muffled voice came through. "Yeah?"

"Hey, could we talk?"

Silence.

"Um, could we do it another time? I'm kinda tired right now," Keegan's soft voice answered.

I frowned. "Okay, but I want us to talk and make sure we're on the same page."

More silence. Then, "Yeah, okay. Later."

I sighed and walked to my room.

I knew I wouldn't sleep peacefully that night.

Whether it was because I worried Keegan didn't feel welcome and comfortable or because I couldn't get the sight of Keegan dancing out of my head, I didn't know. Probably a combination of the two.

But I definitely dreamt of blue silk and lace panties.

TWO

KEEGAN GREER

I GROANED and flopped onto my bed.

Okay, it wasn't really *my* bed. It was Jacob's bed in Jacob's house.

Part of me wanted to march my sexy silk and lace clad ass out of the room, find my host, and tell him he deserved the eye-full he got since he barged in on me. Tell him I'm gay, sassy, and proud and I take no shit from anyone about who I am.

The other part of me realized two things rather quickly. First, that was my personality online and in my head. In *person*? I became a meek and mild, scared of crowds, will do whatever it takes to avoid confrontation, please don't speak to me, coward. No sass, no snark, no standing up and being proud.

Online Keegan was a badass.

Real-life Keegan was a limp noodle.

Second, even if I had the balls to tell Jacob he could just accept me as I am—silk and lace and fabulous gay self—the man was doing me a huge favor by letting me stay. I needed this room, this remote location, this time to finish my schooling. If that meant apologizing to Jacob for what he saw and promising he'd never see that part of me again, I'd do it.

As in, I'd grovel and make promises.

I wouldn't *actually* give up who I was. I'd just make sure the door was always locked and that I kept myself in check around Jacob.

I'd been a fairly timid child, given to flights of fancy and drama. The fancy and drama had only increased as I got older, much to the dismay of my mother. *Too girly. Too prissy. Too dramatic.* Mom always indicated I was too fragile, that I needed to buck up. She hated the colorful me, the makeup-wearing me, the silk and lace me. Needless to say, Mom and I had a tumultuous relationship. She provided me with a place to stay and food, but that was the extent.

Now, don't get me wrong, Mom had a ton of her own issues. But she spent so much time focusing on all of what she thought was wrong with me, she never had time to get help for herself. So, when I found her overdosed in the bathtub, I wasn't even surprised. Shaken, haunted, traumatized? Yes. But to be honest, I was likely all of those things *because* of my mom. Her death just added to my pile of issues.

After Mom's death was when my fear of crowds and going out in public got the worst. I was nearly eighteen, had just graduated from high school, and needed someplace to stay at least until I could legally rent an apartment. Of course, what I would do for a job was a mystery. Without much choice, I contacted the one person Mom had never wanted me to have contact with. Gary "Doc" Wilson. My father.

Upon explaining to the man who I was—and honestly, who takes a stranger at their word and accepts them as their son with open arms—Doc had taken me in without hesitation. And yes, he insisted I called him Doc. Said he didn't know a *Gary*. He drove from Florida and picked me up in Indiana. Said I could stay with him as long as I wanted. Staying with Doc meant whatever shack he could find to rent wherever he decided to point his car for about six months. Then he decided that we needed a real house. We settled with Doc's father, my grandfather Cyrus, in central Indiana. Cyrus was a crotchety old man, but he liked me. When he died not long after we moved in, Cyrus left the house to Doc and a large amount of money to me. Which I could have after college.

I set to work earning an online degree in trauma informed care—what better way to help myself and others than by understanding how trauma affects our brains? All was going great. Doc did a lot of ordering in when he was around—but he traveled a lot. At first, he spent a ton of time with me, but then he got antsy and started taking little trips. He'd have his sister stop in and check on me or make sure the housekeeper came around to keep an eye on me. When Doc wasn't around, I'd order delivery. Sometimes of meals, sometimes of groceries so I could cook for myself.

The few times I needed to go out, I had to psych myself up for it. Always turned out to not be *as* bad as I'd anticipated. Honestly, the anxiety and anticipation were the worst. But I preferred to stay in as much as possible.

That didn't mean I didn't love outdoors. I did. Loved sitting in the sun, soft breeze on my face. I'd take walks as I could, but I got nervous about seeing people and having to make eye contact or even give a small smile. So, I got most of my exercise by dancing. I wasn't a professional, I wouldn't be winning any awards, but I loved it. Add in my silk and lace panties and I was a happy camper.

I'd known I liked guys from a very young age. Despite my mom being very against me, I pretty much just shrugged her off and went about being me. I was accepted at school, but I started online home learning after sixth grade, so I likely missed out on prime bullying years.

Silk and lace had always been textures I loved to have against my skin. I used to secretly purchase ladies' underwear to wear in private until I realized I could buy men's underwear in silk and lace. The cut was much better and allowed for more room up front.

Silk, lace, panties, makeup, dancing, and school all brought me happiness. Oh, and my webcam show made me happy, too. But I'd just recently started that and I wasn't completely sure it would last.

For the time being, donning a mask, pulling on silky panties, and dancing for the camera was all kinds of fun. People paid to watch. They paid more to make requests. And eventually, they'd pay a higher fee if they wanted a private show.

I'd taken a short hiatus from the webcam show when Doc decided to sell Cyrus's place and go on some journey around the world. I liked Doc. He was a good person. Very intelligent and he treated me better than my mom *ever* had. Doc accepted me—well, sometimes I thought his head was so far in the clouds that he didn't even realize I was different. Or maybe he was so different himself that my uniqueness didn't even register. Either way, I liked Doc as a person. As a parent, he was iffy. He wasn't *bad*, but I always got the feeling that having a kid was about ninety-nine on his list of one hundred things he was concerned about at any given time.

I was upset when Doc decided to sell the house. Not so much surprised. And not angry he was leaving. Again. But I had zero desire to traipse across the world with him, especially while trying to earn my degree. Doc's other suggestion of moving in with my aunt, Doc's sister, who lived in fucking New York City, nearly brought me to panicked tears.

So, when Doc said his best friend, Jacob Oakley—whom I'd heard a lot about—was willing to give me a place to stay, it didn't take me long to say yes. Staying with a complete stranger in his very large home in the middle of nowhere Indiana was much better than traveling the world with Doc or dying from a panic attack in New York City.

But now I was living in Jacob's home and it was awkward as fuck.

Sure, I'd made it bad by dancing nearly naked in my new room, but *he'd* made it worse by walking in on me. What the hell? I wasn't embarrassed of my body. I knew I didn't have lots of bulky muscles, but my arms, abs, and chest were somewhat defined. And I had an amazing ass—which was why I loved looking at it and dancing in the sexy panties. Men I hooked up with—okay, *virtually* hooked up with— always complimented me on how soft and smooth my body looked. The one sexual experience I had back before my mom overdosed was as bad of a memory as my mom was so I tried to block it out as much as possible.

The thing with me was I loved love. I loved the idea of being in love. I loved the idea of being loved. I had almost zero experience with love, but knew what I wanted from a loving relationship. And I'd get one. Someday. When I found the right person who could accept the real me and love me for *me*. Until then, I'd continue studying people—human nature was fascinating—reading romance and erotica, watching porn, watching sappy romances, putting on shows for my webcam audience, dancing, wearing my silk and lace, applying makeup every time the mood hit, and learning how to get myself off with the large supply of sex toys I'd ordered online over the past few years.

To say I had nearly zero experience with love and sex was one hundred percent true. To say I was well-versed in relationships—just not my own—was also accurate. To say I was the sluttiest, most self-satisfied, kinky virgin was also spot-on.

Keegan Greer was nothing if not interesting. And I planned to keep it that way. No way I would ever get accused of being boring or plain.

I only wished my outer persona could be as brash and brave as the inner me.

Case in point. Jacob came to my door and wanted to talk.

Inner me wanted to throw open the door, demand that he knock next time he wanted to speak to me, tell him *no way* would I change myself for him, and ask if he'd liked what he saw.

Outer me hid behind the closed door and begged him to wait until the next day. And now I'd toss and turn all night in anxious anticipation of what Jacob might say. Would he be disgusted? Threaten to throw me out if I couldn't control my predilection for silk and lace? I hadn't even worn makeup around him. Would that be a deal-breaker?

Jacob had to know I was gay. Doc was very open about it. He had no problem with my lingerie, makeup, dancing, any of it. To be fair, he wasn't the most observant and had trouble focusing on any one thing, but I knew he'd seen me in makeup and there's *no way* he could have missed my silk and lace hanging to dry on laundry day.

Doc and Jacob were best friends—I had *no* idea how that friendship started, but it seemed long-lasting and genuine— so I was pretty sure my father told Jacob I was gay.

If that had been a problem, surely Jacob wouldn't have let me move in. Or maybe he was one of those *I don't care who you sleep with, just don't flaunt it in my face* type heterosexuals. To be fair, I didn't *know* he was straight, so I shouldn't assume. Inner me wanted to scream *fuck you! I'm here, I'm queer, and I love what I see in the mirror!* Outer me planned to apologize profusely, beg that Jacob let me stay, and just hide in my room even more than I already had been.

As long as Jacob kept having delicious premade meals delivered or making the kick-ass pizza, I'd be set. Study and turn in assignments all day, sneak out for food from time to time, dance for exercise and the endorphin rush, and be the center of attention for my webcam show every night. Something about knowing guys were getting off on me was exhilarating. The thought of having guys getting off *on me* someday also turned my crank. *Hard.* But that fantasy required a lot of things to be in place. Namely, the ability to go out in public and be in a crowd. Kinda hard to make your fantasy of being a cum dump come true when you nearly hyperventilate thinking about being around more than one or two people.

The plan seemed to work just fine in my head. I'd put it into motion tomorrow. Maybe even throw in some times to slip outside and enjoy the gorgeous land Jacob's house was situated on. Yeah, I'd make it work. I only needed a place to stay for a year or so until I could get my degree. By then, I'd have a nice little sum saved up from my webcam show *and* I'd get Grandfather's money. I could rent a tiny apartment and become the hermit I dreamed of being. In today's day and age of online *everything*, I'd never have to leave my place or speak to anyone.

But first, I had to get past the extreme awkwardness of Jacob seeing me almost naked. Maybe I could croak out my apology, get him to agree to letting me stay if I never got caught again, and then rush back to my room without things getting even more awkward.

Maybe.

Hopefully.

Oh God, I was so screwed.

THREE

JAKE

The next morning, I dragged myself from bed after tossing and turning all night. I could *not* get Keegan off my mind. I was embarrassed that I'd walked in on him. I was worried I'd made him uncomfortable. But more than anything, I kept seeing his pale skin, long, thin limbs, and a perfect ass cupped in blue silk.

What the hell?

He was twenty-two. I was forty.

I was his dad's best friend.

And I wasn't gay. Or bi. Or whatever.

Sure about that?

I pushed aside the niggling thought. I wasn't ready to go there. Not now. Maybe not ever.

Not bothering to put on a shirt or change from pajama pants—honestly, I figured I wouldn't see Keegan unless I went to him and pulled him from his hiding place—I shuffled to the restroom to take a piss and then to my office. Setting up my one-cup coffee maker to brew, I went to Bucko's cage.

The damn bird was a menace. He was messy and mouthy. I'd inherited him from an old professor colleague several years ago. Bucko was an asshole if I was being honest. I'd gotten him a very nice cage, kept him supplied with food, water, a mirror, and toys. I cleaned his cage often, talked to him, and made sure his cage was covered when appropriate so he could rest. But all the damn bird did was squawk, curse, and say rude things. His list of words included *fuck*, *fuck off*, *damn bird*, *shut your piehole*. The nicest thing he said was, "What's up, Bucko?" and luckily that was what he said the most often. He sometimes threw in a "Let's go."

Since I lived by myself, it wasn't too big of a deal to have a grumpy asshole bird as a pet. But I always had to be sure Bucko was covered when I was doing online teaching or he'd pepper squawks and curse words throughout my lesson.

As if he knew I was thinking poorly of him, Bucko squawked. Loudly.

"Yeah, yeah," I grumbled. "Good morning to you, too."

"Fuck off," Bucko quipped as he gave me the stink-eye.

I spent a couple minutes making sure he had food and water, but it was obvious he wasn't in a good mood. So, I covered him back up in hopes he would be better later. To be fair, I didn't often wake him so early.

I grabbed my coffee and sat in my comfortable recliner rather than at my desk. I wasn't in the office to work, just to think and try to get my head on straight. About halfway through my coffee, I huffed and sat the mug down. The life-giving beverage wasn't doing it for me.

I leaned back in the recliner and tried to clear my head.

Instead, deep blue silk and lace danced through my mind like damn sugar plums. And then Keegan flitted into the picture. No matter what I did, I couldn't stop seeing the kid in my head. His floppy blondish brown hair, blue eyes, plump ass. And his cock snugged tight against his body by the panties as he moved his body to whatever song played in his ear buds.

Without thinking, I palmed my dick. My very hard dick. *Just morning wood*, I tried to convince myself. I continued to press my palm against my erection as I thought about how I wanted the day to go. I'd give Keegan some time to sleep, then I'd fix a nice lunch from the prepared meals I had delivered. We'd talk. I'd set things right. I'd make sure he knew he was welcome and safe.

And that you're completely fine with watching him dance around his room in silk panties.

I groaned and bit my bottom lip. I needed to stop. It was completely, one hundred percent wrong to be touching myself while thinking about Keegan.

Maybe better to take care of yourself before trying to talk to him? Get whatever strange attraction you've got going out of your head before trying to let him know you're not some old perv and he's safe with you.

I shifted in the recliner and my elbow brushed against the small neck pillow I kept there. The neck pillow that was covered in a damned blue silk pillow case.

Fuck.

As if my hands belonged to someone else, I grabbed the pillow and stripped off the blue silk. At the point of no return —honestly, who was it going to hurt?—I yanked down the waist of my pants, my long, hard cock slapping against my belly, and tucked the elastic under my balls.

Without a second thought—truly, my only thought was of getting off—I wrapped the silk case around my hand and fisted my cock.

Fucking hell.

The silk slid against my shaft, smooth yet providing just enough friction. As I stroked my throbbing dick, I attempted to think of anything other than Keegan. I tried to drum up images of the very few women I'd ever slept with and came up blank. Giving in, I stopped fighting it and pictured

Keegan. I wasn't even sure what I wanted the imaginary Keegan to do, I just jacked off while lusting over his silk-covered ass and dick. When he smiled, batted his lashes, and sucked his bottom lip into his mouth, I lost it. Erupting with a grunt, I spilled hot and thick into the silk pillow case.

"Good morning, I was wondering..." Keegan announced from the door.

Time stood still while also crashing on me in pounding waves.

I blinked rapidly, trying to make sense of what was happening. My spent dick, wrapped in blue silk, in my cum-covered hand. Keegan standing wide-eyed at the door, his words dead on his lips.

Had I not fucking closed the door? Did the kid not know to knock?

Touché.

"Uh, I," I nearly yelped.

Keegan's cheeks were pink and he looked somewhat flustered—not as much as me, but at least a little—but then he cocked his head, narrowed his eyes, and smiled wickedly. "Oh, Professor. This is going to be so much fun." He licked his lips and winked. "I'm ready for that chat whenever you are." Keegan gave a pointed look to my silk covered groin and smirked before walking away.

Holy.

Fucking.

Shit.

How in the hell did I take something already precarious and awkward and turn it into a fiery shit show of epically awkward proportions?

After wiping myself with the now-ruined pillow case, I pulled my pants up, slammed the recliner into its upright position, and shot from the chair. I started a new cup of coffee before stalking to my room where I launched the silk at my laundry basket—too bad silk didn't slam into things when thrown. I growled, yanked on a shirt, pulled on some socks, and slid into a hoodie.

I was fucking pissed at myself and needed to get out of the damn house. I walked to my office to retrieve my coffee and phone.

"What's up, Bucko?" my bird asked.

"Shut your piehole," I growled. Bucko almost never made noises when his cage was covered. Maybe he could sense my terrible mood and wanted to provide comfort. Or the asshole just wanted to rub it in.

After pulling on some shoes I kept in the office, I jerked open the side door that led from my office to the small back garden area. Taking a sip of my coffee, I stood silently for a moment and breathed in the cool morning air. Spring in the Midwest was gorgeous and the chilly morning would likely give way to an amazing afternoon of sunshine and warm breezes.

I took off toward the small woods, anger fueling me and pushing me along. I wasn't angry at Keegan. I was mad at myself.

None of this would have happened if I would have just minded my own business and stayed away from Keegan's room.

Maybe you should have also kept your head out of the gutter and your hand off your dick?

Growling, I pushed a branch out of my way.

I took yet another deep breath and forced myself to think about the whole situation. I was an educated man, I could work this out.

The facts were as follows: having Keegan in the house had thrown me for a loop—I wasn't used to having people around. Keegan, for some strange reason, had pinged an attraction in me that I definitely wasn't ready for. I'd been wrong to wait so long before trying to talk to him and set the stage for our cohabitation.

I could get used to having Keegan there, I just needed some time to adjust.

I couldn't change the fact that I'd waited so long to talk to him, but I could fix that situation. Today.

The unexpected attraction? Well, that may have been what was bothering me the most.

When had I ever been attracted to men?

Really? You're going to pretend you don't remember?

Sometimes I hated my subconscious.

My brain flashed back to a male substitute teacher when I was in first grade. I remembered being totally enamored with him, but surely that was just because I admired and respected him as a male role model. Right?

Another image played through my head as I recalled the teammate I was infatuated with in high school. But that was simply because he was an amazing athlete and I appreciated his skills.

Then there was the classmate I found myself not being able to stop thinking about. He was smart and funny, of course I loved spending time with him.

The neighbor I had before moving to the middle of nowhere? He was lonely and I just enjoyed keeping him company.

Ever have any of those same feelings toward women?

I liked women. Enough that I'd slept with some. A few. Okay, maybe five or fewer.

And the sex was so amazing that you just didn't want to keep at it?

"Shut up," I mumbled to myself. "The sex was fine, we just didn't work out. I'm not the easiest guy to put up with." To be honest, the sex was *fine*, but always left me wondering why everyone thought sex was so great. I'd been a late bloomer and didn't even kiss a girl until college. When I finally had sex, I was definitely confused as to the hype.

A thought crashed through my head. Oh my God, I was eighteen and heading to college when Keegan was born.

Holy. Fucking. Shit.

Not to mention, Keegan's father was my best friend. Doc and I had been friends since we were kids. He hadn't changed at all, still the crazy, flighty, head-in-the-clouds, fly-by-the-seat-of-his-pants type of guy I'd known for what seemed like forever.

"Hey, Doc. So, listen. I walked in on your kid in silk panties," I mumbled to myself and the woods. Hmmm, I wonder if Doc knew about the lingerie. "Yeah, so then I got a boner for your kid. Your kid who is almost two decades younger than me. Oh, and I jacked off thinking about him. About *your son*." I sighed and closed my eyes. I felt like the biggest perv in the world.

What do you think Doc's response would be?

I pinched the bridge of my nose. Doc had been with several women and a few men. Older and younger. He sometimes had multiple partners in one day, sometimes multiple partners at one time. It always made me shake my head. Doc was like the Pied Piper; that crazy hair and wild look in his eyes just seemed to call people to him in droves.

Doc was very openminded. He'd never judge me for being attracted to a man. He wouldn't even judge me being attracted to a much younger man.

But he'd likely have something to say about me being attracted to his son.

As if my thoughts had summoned him, my phone buzzed —scaring the shit out of me in the middle of the silent woods —and Doc's name flashed on the screen.

"Mother fucking hell," I grumbled before thumbing the accept button. "Doc, what's up?"

"Jake-y my man, I miss you. How's that boy of mine? Settling in okay?" Doc's words seemed to be competing with an open window and I smiled as I pictured him driving, his wild hair whipping in the wind, as he screamed over the roar to talk to me.

"He's safe and sound. Pretty sure he thinks I'm a total grump."

"Nah, Keegan is an openminded, free-spirited, quiet thinker. I'm sure he's just grateful for a place to stay and trying to settle in, get his bearings. Why would he think you're a grump?"

Nope, wasn't going into the whole story. "Well, I thought I'd give him time to settle in before we did much interacting, but now he's pretty much holed up in his room and I've not been able to get much out of him." *Yeah, other than interrupting his private dance and blowing your load in front of him.* I gritted my teeth.

"Sometimes with Keegan, his head is his worst enemy. Deep inside, he's this amazing, outspoken, snarky, sarcastic, proud—and so very creative and smart—man, but then he masks it all on the outside. He doesn't love crowds or people in general, but he's longing for love and acceptance. He won't open up until he trusts you and feels like you're worthy of his effort and vulnerability." On the other side, it sounded as if Doc had dropped the phone. "Shit man, I'm going to be late for my rain forest hike. Gotta go. Tell Keeg hi and I love him. I'll call him next chance I get. Love you, man. Thanks for taking care of my boy!"

The line went dead.

Fuck.

Doc did love his kid, but he wasn't exactly high-quality parent material.

Guess you're not either since you're jerkin' off to a twenty-two-year-old.

"Shut the fuck up," I growled.

My coffee was long since gone and I wasn't completely settled with the memories my stupid brain had brought to the surface. But I was determined about one thing.

I would house and protect Keegan. I'd be his friend. A supporter and confidant if needed. Nothing more. He and I could either talk through what had happened or push it under the rug and pretend it never existed. But I was his host and his dad's best friend. Nothing more could or should come from that situation. If needed, I'd work through my own sexuality, but Keegan was *not* going to be a part of that.

Turning toward the house, I walked with a purpose and determination. There would be *no more* inappropriate thoughts about my best friend's son.

Even when he's dancing in silk and lace?

"Shut your damn piehole," I muttered to my head.

FOUR

KEEGAN

I watched through my window as Jacob slammed out of the house. My head and body were all kinds of mixed-up and bothered by this man and the situation. When Jacob had disappeared from sight, I rushed to the kitchen and made a hot chocolate. I knew there was no way I'd be able to avoid the guy forever—and after what I saw earlier, I didn't think I wanted to.

My head maybe wasn't on straight because the weird little thrill I got when I walked in on Jacob jacking off—or right after, but there was *no* mistaking what he'd just done—was spiraling inside me and making me want to do things. Bad things, sexy things, *any* things that would bring that sexed-up, blissed-out, shocked-by-what-he-just-did look back to Jacob's face.

I'd definitely caught him looking me over when he'd barged into my room. Okay, maybe *barged* isn't the right word. I should have locked the door. And he'd probably knocked, I just couldn't hear it over my music. Plus, it was his house.

The fact that he'd jerked off with a piece of silk wasn't

lost on me and did all kinds of things to my insides. But I couldn't push aside the fear that Jacob would be disgusted by what he saw in me and ask me to leave. I was still determined that I'd promise him whatever it took just so I could stay. I *needed* this quiet and protected place to live so I could finish my degree and eventually get the money my grandfather left for me. It wasn't enough money to set me up for life, but it would be a nice start and a nest egg as I began a career. So, if Jacob needed me to hide the real me and never let the sexy, kinky shit out, I'd do that. Hell, it was basically what I did my whole life. I wouldn't change the inner me, but I could play the game and keep the real me hidden around people who weren't comfortable with it. Crappy way to live? Yeah, but it was better than nothing.

Did it look like he was disgusted by what he saw?

I carried my hot chocolate back to my room and curled up on the little window reading nook area. It was my favorite part of the room, so cozy. Jacob had for sure been shocked when he walked in and found me dancing in silk panties.

Dad had never indicated Jacob was gay or bi or anything but straight, but Dad also didn't really have linear thought patterns so him not telling me something wasn't surprising.

I knew Jacob had been shocked when he walked in on me, but he wasn't used to having someone living in his house and probably only expected to find me at my computer working or studying. The fact that he'd later tried to talk to me—in a soft, gentle tone, he hadn't seemed angry—and then jerked off—with *silk* no less—threw me for a loop. Did he have a thing for silk? Did seeing me in silk turn him on?

His shock made sense.

The flicker of shame, anger, guilt, and fire I'd seen dance over his face when I walked in on him—and yeah, I will say I was partly being a bitch by returning that favor—were what really caught my attention. Shame made me think he was not certain of his sexuality or had pushed it aside in hopes of just ignoring it. The anger and guilt were likely directed at himself for several reasons. Angry that he'd walked in on me? Angry and guilty that he was turned on by me? If he even was. Guilty that he'd jacked off to his best friend's much younger son? I could definitely see all of those emotions, especially if his sexuality was in a questioning stage—maybe in a longtime holding pattern.

The flash of fire that I saw was the most intriguing. Was I absolutely ridiculous to think it would be fun to tease and play with Jacob? Was it wrong to want to introduce him to sex with a man, show him how enjoyable kink could be, give him someone to protect and care for physically, emotionally, and sexually? Yes, I was ridiculous and it was wrong. I needed this house to live in. Coming on to my dad's best friend could backfire epically. But that flash of longing and fire were alive and well in my head and I knew it would be difficult to forget them.

So, the guy who has a very limited and very bad history with sex is going to teach a man two times his age how to enjoy sex with another guy? My inner bitch knew how to poke the bear.

"Look," I grumbled to myself, "the bad physical stuff in my past is just that, the past. We were overzealous young teens with zero knowledge and no preparation. Of course, it sucked." I pulled a blanket up over my knees and stared out the window at the beautiful sunny day. "I'm *very* experienced in ways to please myself so I can definitely teach him something about that. I know all about fantasies and kinks. And even if we're talking just good ol' fashioned vanilla sex, I know what feels good. I know I could make things good for Jacob."

If he'd even be interested in you. You're very young, very gay, and very much his best friend's son. That may be very much working against you.

I huffed at my stupid brain.

Before anything, Jacob and I needed to talk. I looked forward to it about as much as someone would look forward to a colonoscopy, but it had to be done. We couldn't spend over a year tip-toeing around each other. Once we'd talked, maybe I could feel out the situation with Jacob as far as him being more than my host.

Did I think we'd become boyfriends and lovers and live happily ever after? No, I wasn't delusional. Was it possible we could have some mutual fun, learn about ourselves and what turns us on, dive into some kinky fuckery, and maybe have a warm body in our bed for the next year? Sure, I wanted to think so.

You seem to forget you've never had anything more than online relationships that basically involved only mutual jerk-off sessions. You also seem to be forgetting that emotions get involved. What if it doesn't work? Where does that leave you?

I ignored the thoughts. For now, the sex idea was just that, an idea. Jacob and I would talk. I'd keep studying and turning in assignments during the day and getting sexy on my webcam at night—it wasn't huge money, but every little bit helped to build my nest egg. Jacob could keep doing his professor shit and whatever else it was he did. The rest of it couldn't be forced; if it seemed like the desire was mutual, we could take things from there.

That hesitant fire and confused longing I'd seen on Jacob's face continued to swirl in my mind and give me hope that the desire was definitely mutual.

I glanced out the window and saw Jacob returning. He looked slightly less tense. I drained my hot chocolate and rushed to jump into the shower. If he wanted to talk, I wanted to be ready and looking my best. I took a deep breath. I was determined to make things different with Jacob. I'd do my best to be real and not hide myself. Unless that was what he needed me to do. I sighed. Damn, I hated when my inside feelings and thoughts didn't match what I was able to present to the outside.

Thirty minutes later, a knock sounded at my door.

"Yeah?"

"Hey, you maybe want to come talk and eat some lunch?" Jacob asked softly from the other side.

I smiled. "Yeah, I'll be there in a minute." The real me wriggled all over on the inside. Maybe Jacob was the right person, maybe he was the one who would allow me to remove my masks and come out to play.

FIVE

JAKE

"JACOB?" Keegan called from the kitchen.

I smiled to myself as I grabbed a bottle of wine. It was nice to hear his voice. "Down here," I answered from the wine cellar, "I'll be right up." I glanced at the bottle in my hand. Was it wrong to give him wine?

He's twenty-two, dumbass. I'm sure he's had a drink. I doubt you're contributing to the delinquency of a minor.

"Hey, you like red or white?" I asked before climbing the stairs. I'd picked a sweet red because it was what I liked best, but I wanted to check with my guest.

"Either, but always sweet," Keegan answered as he peered cautiously down the stairs. "Holy shit, that's like a real wine cellar. I didn't realize those actually existed outside of movies."

Trying to ignore the funny things my stomach was doing when I saw Keegan in full-on makeup, I turned off the light with a laugh and started up the stairs. "Yeah, this house was built by a very pretentious millionaire over one hundred years ago; it has several amenities—even if the layout is a bit unique. The wine cellar may be my favorite." I showed

Keegan the bottle of sweet red and smiled when he smiled. "Sweet is always my go-to as well." I walked to the counter and rummaged for the wine opener. "By the way, please call me Jake. Jacob was my father and we weren't super close. Only stuffy professor colleagues at the college call me Jacob. Friends call me Jake."

The blush on Keegan's cheeks went straight to my cock.

No. Not doing that. Remember?

I wondered when I'd finally give in and work through the old memories and long-ignored sexuality situation.

"Jake," Keegan repeated as if testing the name. "I like it, it suits you better."

I smiled and handed him a glass of wine. "Lunch is in the oven. Should be ready in about five minutes."

"Smells amazing," Keegan said as he breathed in deeply.

I shrugged. "I didn't actually make it, just warmed it up. The meals I have delivered are so good and save me so much time and mess, I just can't give up on the ease and simplicity." I winked. "What I'm saying is I'm a lazy-ass."

Keegan giggled and sipped his wine through plump, pink lips. "This is good." He glanced around the kitchen. "So, you don't cook at all?"

"Well, I have the pizza oven so I use that quite a bit. I make pretty good pizza."

Keegan's thick, black lashes batted over his big, kohl-lined blue eyes. "Yeah, I had a couple pieces. It was good." He bit his lip. "But you can keep the pineapple."

I pulled a face to portray my fake shock. "What?! You don't like pineapple on your pizza? Disgraceful." I shook my head and smiled. "Fine. Next time, you can make your own and do your own toppings."

Why did thinking about making pizzas with Keegan fill me with a happy hopefulness? Damn, had I been this lonely all along?

The timer on the oven buzzed and I removed the lasagna and breadsticks. "There's a salad in the fridge, can you grab it? And whatever dressing you like."

Keegan came to the kitchen island with the salad and a creamy Italian dressing.

"Ah, perfect choice." I grabbed some plates just as a thought screamed through my mind. "Shit, I didn't think to ask. Is there anything you can't eat? Allergies?"

Keegan shook his head and sipped his wine. "No, nothing makes me sick." He smiled teasingly. "Except maybe pineapple on pizza."

When I laughed, he joined in with a light chuckle, and all seemed right in my world.

"You want to eat on the patio?" I gestured to the little covered patio off the kitchen.

Keegan nodded and followed my lead in filling his plate before heading outside.

We settled in at the patio table.

Keegan took a small bite of his salad and hummed appreciatively. Then a bite of breadstick and another hum. After a sip of wine, he dug into the main dish with a bite of lasagna. And he moaned. "So good," he murmured. "Dad wasn't a great cook, so I ate a lot of take-out and frozen food."

I did my best to ignore the feeling in my gut from that moan. "Yeah, Doc could burn water," I teased.

Keegan laughed. "Truth."

"I'm not a great cook, hence the reason I pay someone to make meals for me." I took a bite of lasagna. "It really is good. The chicken potpie is amazing. And the beef stew."

"Oh my God, I'm going to get fat living here," Keegan quipped. But then he froze. "I mean, I don't expect you to feed me. The meals aren't for me. And I'll give you money for like groceries and stuff."

I held up my hand with a gentle smile. "Relax, your dad and I already had this conversation. I pay for meals that are supposed to feed two people, but I swear the lady doubles every recipe. Even with leftovers for lunch or dinner, I always have way too much. There's nothing here that you need to pay for, unless you want something specific thrown into the grocery order."

Keegan hesitated. "Are you sure? I've got some money."

"Stop. It's taken care of. Anything I pay for here is something I'd already be paying for. There's nothing *extra* being charged just because you're here. If you need or want anything, ask. If I don't have it, we can order it." I wrinkled my nose. "Or, if need be, we can go into town and get it."

Keegan giggled. "You like going out in public about as much as me, huh?"

"I kinda hate it. It's not bad if stores aren't super busy, but I get all nauseous and feel faint when it's too loud or too crowded. Sometimes I head into a store, see that it's fairly empty, and spend two hours just browsing the aisles. Sometimes I get there and see it's crowded, turn right back around, and go order whatever I needed online."

"Do you ever feel like you're missing out or sheltering yourself so much that you'll never be able to function in the real world?" Keegan asked with a very serious frown.

I thought about that for a moment. "No, I don't. We live in a time where most everything we could need or want is available for delivery. I have almost daily interaction with colleagues—whether I like it or not—and I spend a lot of time teaching and interacting with my online students. I'm not incapable of social interaction, I just do better when it's on my terms and in small numbers. And for short periods of time. An all-day video call? No thanks."

"What do you teach?" Keegan finished his wine and nodded when I held up the bottle to pour him more.

"My main job is curriculum writing."

Keegan wrinkled his nose. "Is that boring?"

I laughed and shrugged, my cheeks feeling warm with the second glass of wine. "Could be, but I like it. I get to work at my own pace, not have to talk to anyone, and what I write can assure students are learning the important parts of a certain subject or skill."

Keegan cocked his head. "I can see that. It's important, I guess. If not, a bunch of different professors would be teaching a bunch of different things and maybe some are better than others."

"Exactly." I sipped my wine and pushed my plate away. "The other thing I do is teach a couple online classes. I teach the two things I write curriculum for. Freshman level sociology and freshman level writing."

"You like it?" Keegan put his fork on his plate and picked up his wine.

"I do. It can get frustrating dealing with younger students when they don't take things seriously. But I learned quickly that it's not my responsibility to get them to class. If they don't attend and do the work, they don't get the grade. It's easy to spot the kids with a lot of drive, maybe paying for classes on their own, compared to the ones who are there on parents' money and don't really want to be. Or just want it handed to them."

"I can see that." Keegan nodded. "I lucked out and got good scholarships and Dad paid for the rest. I take it very seriously. I love what I'm studying and want to get done as quickly as possible so I can get started building a career."

"Trauma something, right?"

"Trauma informed care. I had to take all the general courses, some extra psychology classes, and I won't be a licensed counselor when I first get out. But I'll be able to use the certificate in trauma informed care to work in group homes and community centers while I work toward becoming a licensed trauma counselor." Keegan smiled and I could see how much he enjoyed it and how proud he was of what he was doing.

"That's great. I'm sure you'll be wonderful."

He wrinkled his nose. "Unfortunately, I have a lot of trauma from the past that I've been able to work through with these courses. But I think my experiences help me to be better at empathizing with and helping others address and deal with their traumas."

We finished our wine in a comfortable silence while enjoying the soft breeze and sunshine.

"You want a tour of the house? I should have offered that the first day, but I told myself you needed time to settle in. I think it was more that I was a nervous wreck and didn't want to mess something up or scare you off." I stood and picked up the dirty dishes.

Keegan nodded and did the same. "It's fine. I probably would have run scared that first night. But I'd love to see the house."

We reached the kitchen and Keegan pursed his lips. "No butler or maid to do the dishes?" he teased.

I laughed. "No. That would require someone being here, under foot, bothering me."

His eyes grew wide and he grimaced.

"No, no. That wasn't in reference to *you*. I barely know you're here." I pointed to the garbage disposal and dishwasher. "I can handle scraping plates and running the dishwasher on my own."

We fell into a quick little process of clearing plates, putting things away, and loading the dishwasher. In less than ten minutes, we were done.

"See? Easy." I hung the hand towel to dry. "So, this house is as odd as the man who built it—at least from what I've been told." I gestured toward the hallway outside of the kitchen. "We'll start upstairs, only because I barely use it."

Keegan followed me up the stairs.

"There's a front stairway and a back stairway. Totally overkill if you ask me." I paused at the top of the stairs. "He had this little sitting area built, but I can't imagine many people gathering at the landing. It's almost as if the house was built to house two families. Perhaps he planned on servants to live up here? Or maybe it was more like an in-laws' quarters? I don't know, but the upstairs is huge. I don't pay to keep it heated or air-conditioned since I'm hardly ever up here. I use it for storage mostly. But if a need ever arose, I'd have three bedrooms and three bathrooms up here ready for company."

Keegan glanced around wide-eyed. "Wow, yeah, an entire family could live up here and just use the kitchen downstairs."

"Oh, that's one of the weird little pieces of this house. Look." I pointed toward a little door in the wall. "This opens to a pulley system with a tray. You can raise and lower it. So, food could be sent up that way."

"Whoa, that's crazy. But kinda genius and convenient."

"There's also a laundry chute that goes from here to the laundry room. So, I really do think he built it with others living up herein mind. Family or servants, I don't know." I started toward the back stairs. "These back stairs aren't as grand and I assume they were built for servants to come and go between the two floors."

Once we reached the downstairs, I motioned quickly toward my studio. "That's a studio, I'm in there a lot. If you ever need me and can't find me in my office, I'm probably in there."

"Studio? For what?" Keegan appeared intrigued.

"Just a wood-carving hobby."

"Oh wow, that's cool. What type of things do you make?" He looked toward the door like he wanted to go in.

I'd never let anyone in my studio. "Decorative things. Special order requests. Canes, pens, figurines, that type of thing."

"Very cool. So, you sell your work?"

I nodded. "Not all of it. Some is just for fun. But I make a decent bit of cash through online sales. Every so often, I'll put some in a local store and let the owner sell them. But I make more online, so I usually stick with that."

Keegan pushed a lock of hair from his forehead. "I'm not all that artistic, so people who do art always impress me."

I frowned and gestured toward his face. "Looks pretty creative to me. And dance, right?" As soon as I said it, my face flushed.

Keegan's cheeks turned a deeper pink than the powdered blush he was wearing. "Yeah, I like to dance." He bit his lip. "The makeup is just fun. I don't do it for pay or for others, it's just for me."

I shrugged. "Well, you're good at it." I moved further down the hall. I wasn't against showing him my studio, but I wasn't prepared. So, I was happy to move away for the time being. "This is my room," I said as I swung open the door to my bedroom.

"Ah, where the magic happens, huh?" Keegan teased, but stuttered over the words before clamping his mouth shut and looking mortified.

I chuckled. "Well, if you mean 'magic' as in trying to sleep —I struggle sometimes—then yes. Can't say there's ever been much *magic* beyond that happening in here."

Keegan cringed. "Sorry, that was dumb. I'm not used to face-to-face conversations with someone other than online and I think my mouth hasn't figured out how to work properly."

I slapped him on the shoulder. "You're fine. I'm sure we'll both have some growing pains."

We walked past the kitchen.

"Over here is one of the two guest bathrooms downstairs. In addition to your room and my room, there are two other bedrooms. Plus, my office. So, in all, seven bedrooms, eleven bathrooms."

"Eleven?!"

"Yeah, every bedroom has a bathroom. So does my office and studio, plus the two guest bathrooms down here. It's crazy." I pointed next to one of the bathrooms. "The laundry room. We can do our laundry together, or you're welcome to wash a load whenever it works best for you."

Keegan, still in awe, just nodded his head.

"Here's my office. You should probably get used to finding me here," I quipped and then recalled just how Keegan had found me there and I couldn't help the groan. "Sorry. Fuck."

Keegan laughed. "We gonna talk about the huge elephant in the room?"

"Probably best if we do," I grumbled. "But first, there's someone I want you to meet." I walked across the room and gently removed Bucko's covering. The bird was old and would sleep as much as I let him, but I liked for him to be awake so he could eat and drink and play a bit. Couldn't be good for an animal to never stimulate its brain. "This," I waved toward the animal, "is Bucko."

"What's up, Bucko?" the bird croaked.

Keegan's eyes went wide and he laughed. "Oh my God, he talks?" He stepped closer to the cage.

"Fuck off," Bucko mumbled.

"Did he…did he just…" Keegan stumbled over the words.

"Did my bird just cuss you out? Yes, yes he did." I rolled my eyes. "He's not going to win any congeniality awards."

"Shut your piehole," Bucko added.

"Well, aren't you just being the show off today?" I laughed at both my bird and Keegan's shocked expression. "He only talks when he feels like it. And I guess he feels like showing all of his talents at once."

"Damn bird," Bucko cooed.

Keegan laughed. "I don't know that I've ever actually heard a bird talk. He's so pretty." He leaned toward the cage. "You're very cool, Bucko."

The damn conceited bird preened, splashed some water, gobbled some food, and then went to murmur noises at himself in his mirror.

I pointed toward the little sitting area. "If I ever held office hours, this is where colleagues and students would sit. But I don't. Partly because I don't want them here. But also because who would want to drive all the way out here?"

"It's quite the trek," Keegan agreed as he took a seat, his eyes flitting toward the recliner.

I was grateful that the pillow was without the silk case for the time being.

"Listen, I'm really sorry for walking in on you," I started, my heart in my chest.

"And I'm sorry for walking in on you," Keegan rushed out the words as he gestured toward the recliner, his ears pink all the way to the tips.

"I shouldn't have barged in and I shouldn't have been doing something so inappropriate in my office."

Keegan frowned. "Look, I should have had the door locked. And it's your house, you can do whatever you want. Nothing was inappropriate, maybe just private." He ducked his head. "My mom hated that I was gay, hated I liked makeup, hated I wore *girly* stuff like silk and lace, hated my dancing. I learned to hide it, keep it from her, so she wouldn't explode in a tirade. I can do the same here. I'm really sorry you had to see that."

I shook my head. "Keegan, you *never* have to apologize for being you. You are who you are. I knew you were gay when your dad asked if you could stay here—hell, I knew you were gay probably the day Doc found out. He was so proud of you and so excited to learn all about his son. The makeup, the dancing, the silk, none of it bothers me." *Definitely doesn't bother me.* I cleared my throat.

Keegan smiled softly. "Thank you. I can see why you and Dad are friends. He's a very open and accepting guy. Not sure how he and Mom ended up together—even if just long enough to make me." He cocked his head. "But you and my dad are also very different."

I laughed. "We're about as different as two people can get, that's for sure."

"So, you're okay with me being gay because you're..." Keegan hedged.

Tension filled my chest. "I'm, um..." I hesitated. I was forty fucking years old, I shouldn't have been unable to answer the question.

"Not sure? Questioning?" Keegan offered. "That's okay. There's no right or wrong timeline. There's no right or wrong label." He shrugged. "Hell, I've known I liked boys since I was young, but that didn't stop me from kissing a couple girls just to be sure." He leaned forward and whispered, "Ten out of ten do *not* recommend."

I couldn't help but laugh as he shivered. "I have always identified as straight. Maybe some past experiences and memories have recently come to light that may make me question that, but I've only ever slept with women. So, straight seems to work." I knew my words were defensive and I felt it in my chest. "For now? Hell, I don't even know anymore."

Keegan was quiet for a while. "Was sex with women amazing?"

I stared at him, unable to answer.

"I'm only asking because the kisses with girls were blah and kinda yucky for me. But kissing boys—before I got too socially awkward and ended up staying holed up at home—was like fireworks. And watching women in porn? I may as well be watching an anatomy video with my old lady Science teacher, Mrs. Moriarity, or watching paint dry—maybe even watching grass grow. It does nothing. But watching the men in porn? It's like a wholly different experience. A feast for the eyes, definitely a turn on." He shrugged. "I'm just saying. Don't ever be afraid to be yourself," he echoed something similar to my earlier sentiment. "You may find that you've been missing out all this time."

I swallowed thickly. "Thanks, I'll, um, I'll take that into account." *So, getting a hard-on and jacking off to the image of Keegan dancing in silk may just be the real me? Awesome. That's not going to cause any issues, I'm sure.*

Keegan gave me a smile that was a mix between understanding and somewhat evil, like the little minx had some kind of devious plan.

SIX

KEEGAN

JAKE—WHO had gone to the kitchen to get us more wine—was a magical creature who twisted my insides and made me simultaneously want to climb him like a tree *and* question every single move I made.

Jake.

His friends called him Jake.

And he wanted me to call him Jake.

Did that make us friends? Were we friends only by association because Doc was Jake's best friend?

Had Jake been questioning his sexuality over a long period of time?

Or did he just start when he saw me in silk? *That* was a heady thought.

He was attracted to me, right? Or was that wishful thinking? Maybe he was just lonely and any hole would do.

Does Jake seem like the type of guy who is just fucking any hole he can find? My brain huffed at me.

If I loved the fact that he wanted me to call him Jake, I absolutely adored the fact that he didn't even blink at my makeup—except to compliment it. He didn't even appear to be forcing it when he said the silk and lace and dancing didn't bother him.

Aside from my dad—and even he was hard to talk to sometimes because he was so flighty and out there a lot of the time—Jake was the first and only person I'd spent any real face-to-face time with in several years. And I wasn't anxious about getting away from him. Wasn't longing to end the conversation. I wasn't even about to die over every single word I said. Okay, maybe every third word, but that was real progress for me.

I could put on a good act with my webcam audience; they never saw my face—I was either filming from chin down or I wore a mask. But Jake was right there, in real life, and I wasn't having a panic attack talking to him. He'd somehow spun some sort of spell around me—and I was a thousand percent sure that he had no idea he'd even done it—so that I could talk to him, let down the walls, be the real me.

Jake was an enigma—he had the same social anxiety as me, yet he relaxed me and it seemed I did the same for him. I'd never met anyone like him. He was a treasure—I felt dumb even thinking that, but even in the short amount of time I'd known him I recognized that Jake was different. Jake made *me* different. I wasn't sure how or why, but I was already different with him than I'd been with anyone else.

Sure, I could play with the online viewers, but this was a real person. Real feelings. Real butterflies in my stomach around him. And—as crazy as it felt to say it—a real connection despite only just meeting him.

Part of me—the part I showed to the outside world— wanted to reach out, claim Jake as a friend, and bask in the happiness we could find in that friendship.

The other part of me—my inner sexy, kinky minx— wanted to tease him, play with him, bring him out of his hidey-hole when he was ready. I wanted to introduce him to so much, wanted to share all of me with him. The fun we could have in bed was limitless and the prospect had me wiggling in my seat.

As I watched Jake return from the kitchen, two glasses in hand and the remaining bottle under his arm, I wondered silently if there was any hope of having it all. A friendship, a relationship, and the sexual fulfilment I imagined Jake and I could bring to each other.

I had no issue picturing all of the things I wanted to do to Jake—and all of the amazing things Jake could do to me. I imagined dropping to my knees to suck his cock between my lips, deep to the back of my throat, while I fondled his balls. I'd be the first to do that for him. I'd never participated in rimming, but I wanted more than anything to spread Jake open and tongue his hole. Would he ever want to do that to me? Kissing, stroking, licking, and biting were all things I wanted to do—all things I wanted us to do together. I dreamed of stretching myself with a toy so Jake could slowly remove it and fill me with his cock—which of course would be big and beautiful because it was my fantasy and I could imagine his cock any way I wanted to. Would Jake ever want his ass played with? Would he tie me up? Choke me? Spank me?

Would Jake ever be able to understand my kinkiest fantasy? If we were friends and lovers, would he want to give me that fantasy? Or would it be too much? Too out there? Too over the top for him?

Damn, Keegan. Maybe you should figure out if the guy even wants to kiss you before you think about him providing you with a cum dump scene.

I coughed and took the glass of wine Jake held out to me.

"You know, I was just thinking of the craziness Doc and I used to get into."

I smiled. "I'd love to hear stories about you and my dad."

I'd also love to have you as my daddy—spanking me, drawing pleasure from me, taking care of me. I cleared my throat. Fuck. I had to get my head together or I'd end up with a major boner right in Jake's office.

He laughed. "Doc has *always* been given to flights of fancy. He's never been what I'd call a grounded person. Flighty, free-spirited, heart-of-gold? Definitely. Planner? Organized? Realistic? Never."

I giggled before sipping my wine. "Sounds like Dad."

"We used to make up these great games to play and Doc would last maybe fifteen minutes into the game and then he'd be off on some wild new idea." Jake chuckled to himself. "I always wanted to spend hours playing the game we'd just created, but Doc would convince me to switch to his newest story or game. I've never known why, but saying no to Doc is something I've never been good at."

I snorted and gestured toward my chest. "Hence the reason I'm sitting in your office right now."

Jake shrugged. "Wasn't even something I considered saying no about. But even as kids, Doc had a power of persuasion over me. Not that he ever asked me to do anything *wrong*. Sometimes his ideas were a little half-baked and we ended up in some precarious situations where we had to do a lot of explaining. Or a lot of praying that we wouldn't end up losing a limb."

It was hard to picture my dad as a child. "How did you guys meet?" I asked.

"We were neighbors. Friends from before we even started school. Back then, parents would send their kids out to play and not expect them back until dusk. One of our moms would set some bologna sandwiches, cheese balls, and red Kool-Aid on the back step. We counted ourselves lucky on days they both set out food. If my mom was feeling generous, she'd give us each a pudding pop. Doc's mom always had those twin popsicles. We liked orange the best." Jake smiled fondly at the memory. "I can still taste those cheese balls. They still make them, but they aren't the same these days. Probably had to take all the bad shit out of them."

Jake spent a few more minutes telling me stories about him and Doc. Bike wrecks, scraped knees, daring to walk through the big sewage tunnel under the road, using magnifying glasses to start fires, chasing snakes, and even learning to hotwire a car as teens.

"I love that you and Dad have such a long history and great memories," I said with a sigh. "I don't really remember friends from my childhood."

Jake snorted. "You're still a child."

I frowned. "Don't do that. Please? I'm one hundred percent an adult. Legal in all aspects. I may be younger than you, but I'm not a child." Holy shit, where had that little burst come from? It had been *years* since I'd voiced my opinion to someone face-to-face.

Jake sobered. "I'm sorry. I didn't mean to be offensive."

"It's just that I want you to see me as an equal, not as a kid." I waved it off. "I got along with kids at school fine. But then my social anxiety started getting worse and worse. Mom had me start doing online courses because she was sick of my worries over going to school." I pursed my lips. "She was also sick of my girly shit, my dancing shit, pretty much just sick of me."

"She had a lot of issues," Jake offered softly. "When Doc found out about you, he told me about her—after he spent hours telling me all about you and how excited he was to have a son. Your mom had an untreated mental illness and her behavior and death weren't your fault. You know that, right?"

I swallowed thickly. "In theory? Yes. But that doesn't change the fact that she pretty much doted on my sister and despised me. And doesn't make it any easier every time I remember finding her dead." I closed my eyes and took a deep breath as I pushed away the image. "My sister looked at me the way Mom always had—plus, she was older so she'd already moved out and was on her own. She wasn't coming back to help me. Teenagers shouldn't have to deal with dead bodies."

"I'm sorry, Keegan. Nobody should have to experience that."

I smiled. "I know. I'm working through it—I probably will be working through it for a long time." I drained the rest of my wine and handed the glass to Jake when he reached for it. I watched him as he poured me another full glass. Jake was not the typical buff, macho guy I'd usually go for. His dark hair was graying at the temples, his hazel green eyes framed by dark lashes and slight crows-feet when he laughed. He was taller than me by about four inches, outweighed me by about fifty or more pounds, and had a definite *dad-bod* which I'd never thought I'd find attractive but he had me nearly drooling. He wasn't fat, but there was no mistaking that Jake didn't spend hours a day in the gym.

And all I wanted to do was strip him naked, lick his nipples, rub my nose against his slight belly, and let him feed me his cock inch by glorious inch.

"Keegan?"

I startled out of my day dreaming to find Jake, brows raised, holding out my wine glass.

"Sorry, I was out of it for a moment." I took the glass and swallowed a large amount.

We spent another hour finishing the wine and talking about my dad and Jake as kids. I wasn't sure when I'd had a more enjoyable day.

∿

I PERCHED on the kitchen counter, legs swinging from under a purple silk robe, and watched as Jake made coffee for himself and hot chocolate for me.

Over the past few weeks, we'd settled into a comfortable routine and I adored it. I spent most of my mornings in a tank, silk panties, and a silk robe. Partly because it was super comfy and I loved the softness of the material against my skin. Partly because I was a flirty tease who got a little thrill out of provoking Jake.

Maybe I wasn't even affecting him. Maybe I was just kidding myself. But I swore I caught his eyes on me more than once.

Jake was an early riser, but the scent of his first cup of coffee and his clanging around in the kitchen would wake me. I'd stumble to the kitchen all rumpled and bedhead-y and take in the glorious sight of a showered and put together Jake. We usually chatted a bit while he made breakfast—usually eggs and toast—and after a couple days of me making myself a hot chocolate, Jake just started making it for me. By the time breakfast was ready, Jake would be on cup number two of his nasty black coffee, and we'd settle in at the little breakfast nook.

Breakfast with Jake was one of my favorite times of the day. We'd chat and read the paper. He got an actual newspaper delivered every morning—had to pay an extra delivery fee for the distance—and we fell into a habit of leaving phones on the kitchen counter while we ate, read the paper, and lingered over Jake's third cup of coffee. Then we'd part ways and both go off to work and study.

By the time lunch rolled around, I was always sure to have showered. While I wasn't the type to do my hair and makeup *only* for Jake—let's face it, I liked the way I looked and did it just as much for myself—I did often think about him on the days when I decided I wanted to put on a full face. My usual daytime attire was boring boxer briefs, a tank or t-shirt, and jeans or sweatpants. Funny thing, I caught Jake staring at me just as often in the jeans or sweats as he did when I wore the sexy silk robe.

"You have any big projects due soon?" Jake asked as he handed me a mug of hot chocolate.

"Already turned it in. I like to be early with assignments. Class is pretty light from now until the end of the month."

"Same for me. Just lots of students finishing up projects and turning in papers. Luckily, I have assistants to grade most of the assignments; they only send something my way if they aren't sure about a grade." Jake put the bread in the toaster. "Can you get the butter?"

We continued our easy conversation as we carried our food to the tiny table.

"Since you're not super busy, I was thinking maybe you'd want to help me plant a garden? Maybe do some landscaping?" Jake took a bite of eggs.

"As in outside in the heat? With bugs and sweat?" I wrinkled my nose.

Jake chuckled. "Why am I not surprised that you don't love the great outdoors?"

"Oh, I love the great outdoors. I'd just rather sit in the shade with a cool drink and enjoy nature than be out *in* it. Eeeww." I watched Jake for a moment. "*But* I could possibly be persuaded to join you in this hellish manual labor in exchange for a favor." I batted my lashes, knowing damn well they looked sultry against my dewy pink cheeks and smoky eyes.

Jake's eyes went wide and I would have *loved* to know just what *favor* he thought I was going to ask for. *Very good information to know*, I thought to myself. Jake had ideas about favors, they appeared to be somewhat sexual, and he could possibly be persuaded to trade favors. *Very interesting.*

"Um, I don't know, um, what kind of favor exactly?" Jake stumbled over the words.

My knee bumped against his and I nudged my shoulder into him. "Stand down, Professor. I'm not offering *those* kinds of favors. *Yet*." I winked. "How about I help you and you show me your studio?"

Jake blinked at me for several seconds. "Oh. Um, yeah. I could probably do that. I mean, it's not very exciting. Probably. Not even worth a couple hours sweating in the sun."

"Well, my physical contribution will likely not even equal a couple actual hours of work, so it's all good," I teased.

"You want to work on it today? Weather's supposed to be great." Jake eyed me with a hopeful gleam in his eyes.

I narrowed my eyes. "Can you give me a bit more detail about what I may be agreeing to?"

He laughed. "We'll start small. Go into town," he began.

I balked.

"You don't have to go. Just thought getting out of the house might be nice. I go to a little garden shop. They leave me alone unless I'm asking specific questions."

I nodded. "Okay, go on."

"I'm wanting to get my little garden area ready and planted. Plus, maybe do some potted plants. I can wait on the landscape. Actually, I even thought about just hiring someone to do that part." Jake raised a brow. "What do you think? Can you ride to town, help me plant a garden, and pot some plants?"

The thought of going to a store usually gave me anxiety, but the fact that Jake was going to be with me seemed to dampen that feeling. "Let me grab my shoes."

Twenty minutes later, I was in Jake's beat-up old truck with a hoodie zipped over my tank and the window down just enough so that my hair whipped in the wind. "Oh shit," I gasped, "I didn't even think about my makeup. Will it be a problem? I can stay in the truck."

Jake placed a firm hand on my shoulder. "You're fine. I'd never ask you to change who you are and I wouldn't take you anywhere you'd be unsafe. They likely won't notice and if they do, they won't care."

I took a deep breath and let out a long sigh. "Okay. Thanks." I immediately missed his warm touch on my shoulder when he looked shocked and pulled his hand away.

The little garden shop was adorable and I decided I'd never turn down a trip into town if it meant a visit to the shop.

"Oh my God, I wish I'd thought to bring money. Look at how fucking cute these are," I exclaimed and grabbed Jake's arm to drag him toward the display of fairy gardens. "If we come back, can I buy a few and put them somewhere? I won't make it gaudy and no one else will be able to see it. Maybe outside my window?"

"Pick out any of the pieces you want."

"I can't afford that much, but I could pay you back for a few." I hated the thought of owing anyone money.

Jake smiled. "Well, pick the ones you want for now."

I quickly picked five pieces that would make an adorable little fairy garden.

A soft hand landed on the small of my back. "Just for fun, if money were no object, which ones would you pick to add to your garden?"

I spent about five minutes pointing to pieces and telling Jake why I'd pick each extra piece. Leaning into his touch, I hefted my little shopping basket. "Thanks for spotting me on these. I'll give you money as soon as we get home." Was it weird that Jake's place seemed so very much like *home* already?

Seeming to like my answer about *home*, Jake smiled. "I'm

not worried. Now, come help me pick seeds, plants, and flowers."

An hour and a half later, we climbed into the truck after loading the bed with all of our purchases. For the garden, we had green bean, zucchini, cucumber and cilantro seeds, and tomato and pepper plants. Jake had picked a colorful array of potted plants that he wanted to transfer to his own pots and build specific arrangements. He seemed to have an image in his mind of what he wanted this to look like.

"I've never had a garden," I rambled. "I love fried zucchini. Oh, and zucchini noodles. Maybe we could make salsa?" I paused. "We didn't get anything to grow onions. Can you grow avocados?"

Jake laughed. "I've created a monster."

"No worries, I won't be so excited when it's time to plant all of this."

"We'll definitely make salsa this summer. We can buy onions and avocados at the little farmers market. Or I'll have it delivered in my grocery order." He smiled my way. "Zucchini noodles are amazing. We'll feast all summer."

I smiled. My brain felt a bit overstimulated from the trip to town, but I was so damned happy I couldn't even complain. "I'll help you with all this first, but I definitely want to set up my fairy garden. Where do you think the best place would be?"

"I think there's a perfect place outside your bedroom window—if that's where you want it—there's a little grove of bushes that would work great," Jake said before climbing out of the truck once we'd driven up his long, winding lane. "But first, we do the garden. Then lunch to rest my old bones. Then the potted plants. *Then* we'll do your fairy garden."

Three hours later, I straightened up from a crouched position, wiped sweat from my brow, and groaned. "Oh my

God, *why* did you have to put the garden *right* in the middle of the damned sun?"

Jake laughed. "Plants need sunshine, Keegan." He narrowed his eyes at me and adjusted the hat perched on his head. "You need some more sunscreen."

I'd long since tossed my hoodie to the side due to the heat—okay, it definitely wasn't the hottest day I'd ever experienced, but it wasn't cool and comfortable. And I'd smeared some sunscreen on my shoulders, neck, and nose before taking the floppy hat Jake offered. "You put it on me, please. I can't reach the back of my neck so well." I batted my lashes—which I *knew* were smearing mascara all over my sweaty face. "Dear Lord in Heaven, please forgive my little gay ass for the atrocity that I am at this very moment," I whispered.

Jake grabbed the sunscreen and busted out laughing. "What the hell are you mumbling about over there?" He flipped the lid and began smoothing the warm lotion all over my shoulders, neck, and upper back.

"I've committed a sin. Proper ladies and gays are *not* supposed to sweat—we *glisten*. But I've gone and bulldozed right past glisten straight to sweating buckets. My makeup is beyond repair. I'd likely scare small children. The mascara streaks may *never* wash away—I'll be left with the daily physical reminder of my transgressions." I put the back of my hand to my forehead. "My only hope of pardon is the fact that I'm helping the elderly," I quipped as I turned to face Jake with a huge, cheesy smile.

"Hey! Low-blow, kid. Low-blow." He handed me the tube of sunscreen. "I don't think you really need any more on your face. The floppy hat is covering it all." He leaned in to whisper. "And, mascara sins or not, I think your face looks absolutely adorable." Then he turned to continue pulling weeds from the dirt.

I stood there, mouth agape, for what seemed like hours. Let it go? Call him out? Maybe it was the thrill of shopping with Jake or the excitement over a fairy garden for my wee fairy self or maybe the sun had baked my brain, but I couldn't just let it go. I returned to making a long row in the dirt and dropping in green bean seeds like Jake had shown me. After about five minutes of comfortable silence—perhaps only slightly laced with a tremor of tension—I couldn't wait any longer.

"So, you think I'm adorable?" I leaned on the hoe and popped a hip. "I mean, I'm a sweaty, dirt-and-mascara-streaked mess. I likely stink to high heaven. This hat is doing *nothing* for my look. But you still think I'm adorable?" I bit my lip trying to hide my smile. It did crazy weird things in my chest to think Jake thought I was cute.

Jake narrowed his eyes. I could almost see him mentally calculating what he'd said to lead me to what *I'd* said. Then he seemed to realize his slip-up. He took a deep breath and let it out slowly. "Look, that probably came out wrong. I wasn't like hitting on you or anything. I'm sorry."

"What if I told you I wouldn't be at all offended if you *were* hitting on me?" I shifted the pole in front of my body and positioned it as if it were a dance pole. "What if I told you I love that you think I'm adorable?"

Jake cleared his throat. "I'd, um, I'd…" He coughed. "I'd think there's *way* too much in this whole situation to process. Plus, we have gardening to do. So, let's forget the conversation even happened." He stabbed a shovel into the ground and began planting the first of six tomato plants.

I smiled and finished the row of beans. We'd have two long rows once the plants began to grow. Jake said he usually kept half for fresh veggies throughout the summer and canned half so he'd have plenty of greens during the winter.

As we approached the end of putting out the garden, I decided to plant one more seed. "Just so you know. I'm attracted to you. I've been plenty of straight guys' dirty little online secret, and I'd be that for you, but I don't think that's what it would be for you. I think you're definitely questioning your sexuality. Probably long before I showed up—but I brought things crashing to the front of your mind. I may not have a ton of real-life, physical experience with other men, but I have a wealth of knowledge about what feels good, how to please a man, and plenty of personal experience with toys and pleasuring myself. If you ever have questions, want to know how something works, want to try something, just let me know. I'm not delusional enough to think someone like you would ever want a real relationship with someone like me, but I'd be more than happy to help you learn. We could both get a lot of enjoyment from each other. It's a looong time before I'm done with classes and out of your hair."

Jake likely tasted the dirt after he picked his mouth up from the ground. "Um, wow." He frowned. "First, don't ever think that *someone like you* isn't worthy of a loving relationship. But we've got way too much working against us. You're much too young. Your *dad* is my best friend." He kinda shivered. "And what if I try something and realize I'm *not* gay or bi or whatever? I'd never want to hurt you or make you feel like some dirty little secret."

I sauntered my sweaty, stinky self over to Jake. "If you can one thousand percent tell me that the thought of me dropping to my knees right here in the garden and sucking your cock until you're coming down my throat doesn't turn you on in the least bit, I'll forget this conversation ever took place." I was close enough to feel the heat from his body. "But I get the distinct feeling that you would be completely turned on by the image of me, bent over, my silk-covered ass up in the air, legs spread wide, while your cock slid into me hard and deep. Am I right?"

Jake swallowed so loud I heard the click of his throat. "Let's get lunch," he grumbled and walked toward the house.

"That's what I thought," I mused as I watched his fantastic jean-clad ass stomp away from me. "No worries, Jake. This will be oh-so-much fun. We'll go slow, I promise. Just let Keegan take care of you."

After we'd both washed up—and I had been right, my face was an absolute mess—we sat down at the little kitchen nook to eat sub sandwiches and chips. Jake chuckled at the face I made when I sipped the iced tea.

"Sugar or sweetener is in the cabinet. Why am I not surprised you want your tea sweet as syrup?" He took a long sip of his dirt water—sure, he *called* it iced tea, but it tasted like dirt. "Ah, refreshing."

"It's bitter and tastes like dirt," I retorted as I put several packets of sweetener into my glass and stirred. I took a long sip. "Ah, delicious."

Jake just chuckled and shook his head.

Deciding I'd take it easy on him, I started a more neutral conversation. "So, you have a mental image of what these potted plants are going to look like?"

He nodded. "Yep, I've got four huge pots and a layout ready for which plants I want in those. I've got four hanging baskets and I know which plants I'm putting in those. The remaining plants we'll put in longer window-sill planters for outside my bedroom, your bedroom, and the kitchen so we can always enjoy some flowers."

"Sounds perfect. Just show me what you want me to do." I popped a chip in my mouth.

"You'd agree to just about anything right now if it meant getting to your fairy garden sooner rather than later, I think," Jake said around a bite of turkey and cheese.

"You're not wrong." I smiled and shrugged. "Make sure I give you the money later. I can transfer it to you if you have PayPal or similar. And maybe next time we go to the garden shop, I can get a few more pieces." I wasn't broke, but I knew it was best to put as much of my money aside for the future rather than blowing it on fairy gardens.

Jake gave a non-committal grunt and gathered up our trash. "Drink a bottle of water before we go back out. We'll mostly be in the shade for planting now, but you don't want to dehydrate."

An hour later, Jake had shown me his designs for the potted plants and we'd donned gloves and dug in. I'd never planted seeds or plants before, never really been an outdoorsy type, but I found I loved having my hands in the soil. Knowing that I was potting a plant that would later bloom and provide oxygen and beauty for those around it made me feel good.

When we were done, Jake had me help move the four huge planters to the front and back patios. Two hanging baskets went to the front and two to the back. We finished by attaching the window-sill planters to all three windows before standing back to admire our work.

"They all look amazing," I said.

Jake agreed and then gestured toward the garden. "And they'll taste amazing as well."

"Thanks for letting me be a part of this. It was fun. Mom definitely never had a garden. Hell, she likely refused to have one thinking it would make me more gay or something. Dad likes farmers markets, but he's not around enough to take care of a garden or plants." I glanced at the side of the house. "Can you show me where you think the fairy garden should go?"

Jake smiled and led me toward my bedroom window. He was right. Directly in front of my window was a tiny grove of bushes with a small area that would be perfect for the little set up.

"This is great! I'll be able to see it from my reading-nook." I brushed aside some of the debris.

"If you'll let me break up some of this dirt, I think we can plant some flowers around the edge and your buildings and figurines can go in the middle," Jake offered. "I think I even have another short pot and maybe some edging that you could use to add dimension."

"Perfect. I'm going to grab the bag if you want to break up the dirt."

"Yeah, just let me get the tools, supplies, and the extra flowers." Jake nodded and headed toward the garden area.

When I returned with my bag of purchases, Jake was bent over, his strong shoulders pulling against the t-shirt as he tilled the dirt.

We chatted a bit as we put some of the flowers into the earth and some into the extra planter and watered them. They'd get rain in this location and just the right amount of sun.

I dug into my bag just as Jake picked up a second bag.

"Oh, I think we somehow got home with extras," he said with a wink.

I took the bag he held out and gasped when I saw what was inside. Basically, every single piece of the fairy garden I'd pointed out were boxed and packed into the bag. "Jake, no, you can't buy me all of these. And I definitely can't pay for all of them."

"Do you like them?" Jake asked, seemingly ignoring my protests.

"Of course, I adore them. But it's too much."

"Nah, consider it my house warming gift to you as a move-in present." He winked.

"I moved into *your* house. It doesn't work that way," I argued.

"Get busy opening those boxes. I want to see how you set it up."

My mouth gaped like a damn dying fish. "It's too much," I tried again.

Jake just waved me off. "I'm going to clean up around the garden and look into hiring out the rest of the landscaping. I'm too old for this shit."

I glanced over my shoulder. "I think your age looks really good on you." I winked and Jake blushed.

"Holler when you have it completed. I want to see." He gave me a smile framed by pink cheeks.

With that, Jake left me alone to unbox all of the pieces like a kid on Christmas morning. Each box brought me more joy and I was nearly bouncing with excitement by the time I set to work placing all of the pieces.

Over an hour later, I'd determined that I may have been a bit obsessed with my fairy garden *and* putting one together wasn't a job that would likely ever be *done*. I could definitely see me constantly wanting to add to it, change things, spruce it up.

But I stood back and took in my work. I'd done a good job. My hands were a mess from digging in the dirt, but I'd managed to use some of the edging to build a tiny pond. I liked the look of the tiny rock wall nestled among the flowers we'd planted. The tiny mini waterfall fell to a brook that flowed past one of the miniature fairy abodes. I loved the height the planter added, and used it for another house plus a wooden staircase leading down to the main part of the area.

I definitely wanted to add twinkling lights. I wondered if I could order some online. And I had enough leftover pieces that I immediately began planning an indoor garden. Perhaps in a succulent planter.

For the time being, though, I was happy. I loved the way it looked. I loved that *I* had built it. I loved that Jake didn't even bat an eye when I said I wanted to make a fairy garden. And a very swirly warmth filled my chest when I recalled Jake had made my little project possible.

My mom had taken just enough care of me to not get turned into the authorities. Doc took me in, got to know me, provided for me, but he wasn't the most nurturing person on the planet. But Jake? Jake seemed to truly care about me. He made sure I had food and shelter. Got me out of the house. Bought things for me. I realized it sounded shallow that I'd think someone cared about me just because they bought me a fairy garden, but very few people had ever bought me something just because they knew I wanted it.

Doc got me a car because I needed it and he was trying to be the cool parent. Guys on the internet had given me gifts and such, but only because they wanted to see my dick or ass. One time my mom bought me a game for my second-hand computer, but that was because she was trying to keep me quiet after the backhand she'd delivered to my face when I'd been a bit too snarky for my own good.

Jake wasn't trying to buy me. He had nothing to keep me quiet about. He wasn't trying to prove he was cool. He didn't want in my pants. Okay, I think he wanted in my pants, but I didn't think *he* knew that part yet—or hadn't allowed himself to admit it. Jake bought the extra fairy garden pieces just because he knew they'd make me happy.

And the pieces *did* make me happy. But Jake's kind gesture meant more to me than the garden figures ever could.

"You done?" Jake's deep voice broke into my silent reverie.

"Shit, you scared me." I put a hand to my heart.

"Seemed deep in thought. Something wrong with the garden?" Jake frowned. "Looks amazing to me."

I smiled. "No, nothing wrong. Just kinda in love with the whole thing." I gestured toward my little creation. "I want to get some twinkly lights and twist them throughout. I also thought about taking these leftover pieces and doing something in a planter indoors."

"Succulents would be good, I think," Jake mused.

"That's *exactly* what I was thinking."

We spent a couple minutes admiring the garden. Well, Jake admired while I talked a mile a minute about the different features and why I put which piece where.

"This looks great. You did a wonderful job."

Without more than a nanosecond of thought, I moved toward him until the lingering heat of our hardworking bodies mingled between us. "Thank you for buying them for me," I whispered and glanced up to meet Jake's eyes.

He swallowed and nodded. "Not a problem. Glad you enjoyed them."

I reached up, my hands lingering only a moment on his chest, before wrapping my arms around his neck and hugging him tightly. "It was the nicest, most genuine gift anyone has ever given me." I tucked my face against his chest. "Seriously, I love it."

Jake froze for moment. Just when I thought he was going to let me be the only one hugging, his arms wrapped around my back and squeezed.

"You're welcome. It's good to see you happy," he answered gruffly.

We stood for several moments, wrapped in each other's arms, and just enjoyed the physical contact. A realization of epic proportions hit me like a Mack truck. My mother had never been a hugger. Doc was a sporadic, one-arm hugger. A couple childhood friends and I would hug on occasion. The few guys I'd made out with—well, there was physical touch there, but not actually *hugs*. And the one disastrous sexual experience I'd had in real-life had definitely not included hugs.

I was starved for physical touch and the anonymous sexual encounters across cyber-space weren't cutting it. I enjoyed what I did, but nothing would ever compare to the warm arms wrapped around me at that moment. Maybe that was why I loved the different textures of silk and lace. Maybe that was why I got off on touching myself for others to watch. Maybe that was why I never wanted to be out of Jake's arms ever again.

"Sorry, just coming to the conclusion that it's been a very long time since I've hugged anyone and I've obviously missed it," I mumbled against Jake's chest.

His arms tightened and a hand ran up and down my back. "Same here. Didn't know how starved I was for it, but it's like I don't want to let you go."

"We should start our own little hug therapy," I suggested.

Jake chuckled.

"I'm serious. I've heard that hugs make people happier and healthier. We should make sure we hug morning, noon, and night. Nice, long hugs like this one. None of those fake one-arm hugs or hugs that last point two seconds." I lifted up on my toes and tipped my face so my lips grazed Jake's neck. "It would be good for our well-being."

Jake huffed and pulled away. "I'm fine with hugs, but I can't say my well-being would benefit. I think it may make me lose my mind."

I sucked my bottom lip between my teeth. "Why, Professor, I do believe you're blushing under that fine sheen of sweat and dirt. Hugs don't *have* to be sexual."

Jake rolled his eyes and turned toward the house mumbling something to himself that I swore sounded like *Tell that to my dick.*

I smiled, threw one last glance toward my little masterpiece, and followed.

We walked into the house through his office door and kicked off our shoes.

"Hiya, Bucko," I said as I approached his cage.

"What's up, Bucko," the bird chirped.

"Oh, you know, planting a garden, getting sweaty, hugging a hot guy," I answered.

"Shut your piehole," Bucko said.

I laughed. "Good talk, bird. Good talk."

Jake chuckled and rolled his eyes. "He's not the most loving pet in the world, that's for sure."

"I like him. He has character."

"You want to shower?" Jake asked.

"With you?" I countered.

He sputtered. "No, in your own shower."

"Darn," I teased. "But yes, I do. I know I stink. Plus, I feel disgusting."

"Something light for dinner? I think I've got some grilled chicken. Could do a salad and breadsticks?"

"Sounds perfect." I licked my lips. "Got any wine to go with that?"

Jake smiled. "Of course."

"Okay. Shower, dinner, and then..." I paused with my brows raised. "Don't pretend like you forgot. I helped plant the garden, now I get to see your studio."

Jake narrowed his eyes. "I actually *had* somewhat forgotten about that little manipulation."

I popped a hip and planted a fist on it. "Do not think you're getting out of it. I want to see what you make."

He rolled his eyes. "Fine. A deal is a deal. But it's really not that spectacular. Just a bunch of wood pieces and a mess for the most part."

"I don't care. I want to see it." I sauntered off to shower.

"Fuck off," Bucko called out.

"Same to you, Bucko!" I hollered back.

AFTER DINNER, Jake and I cleaned up the kitchen and started on a second bottle of wine.

"Do you drink wine often or am I quickly depleting your supply?" I asked as I sipped the sweet red liquid. It was heavier than the white we'd had with dinner.

"I drink a bottle every couple of days. No worries. I've got plenty and I can always order more. I usually have a large order of wine delivered about once a month." Jake took a drink. "Ah, this is a good one."

"How am I so exhausted?" I murmured as I leaned against the counter.

"Well, we went into town and spent all day working in the sun and fresh air. Plus, we're on our second bottle of wine. It makes sense."

I took another drink and nodded. "Well, lead on, Professor. I need to see the studio before I crash."

Jake smiled softly and started toward his studio. "It's really nothing spectacular. I don't want you to be disappointed." He swung open the door.

I walked in and immediately fell in love with the feel of the room. And the smell was amazing. Even with my eyes closed, I'd be able to pick up the scent of wood. But there was also the smell of something else. Resin? Lacquer? And maybe the metal of Jake's tools.

"Oh my God, I love it here." I stood in the middle of the room and turned around slowly. "It's perfect. I love the smell. It's cool and soft and dark." I ran a hand over the back of a small couch. "I could just come here and sleep."

"You're welcome anytime." Jake looked around the studio. "It's a great little space."

"Show me your art," I demanded and walked toward what I assumed was a work space.

"I do a lot of different types of pieces. Some are very rough-hewn. Some I sand down so they are smooth. Some are unfinished by personal preference or request, some I seal with a shiny or matte lacquer. Some pieces are left a natural color, some get a varnish." He held up different pieces to illustrate what he was saying.

"What type of wood do you use? Are some types better than others?"

Jake shrugged. "Beginners usually do best with basswood or aspen. Butternut is also good. Black walnut is great, though it's a bit more expensive. It's got a rich color and nice grain. Oak is very strong and sturdy, so it's great for furniture."

"Do you make furniture?" I asked.

"No, haven't ventured that far into the hobby yet. I stick mostly to small to medium pieces of the decorative variety." Jake pointed to animal figurines, a tiny boat, a person who looked like a fisherman, a picture frame, a small box, a bowl, and a rectangular piece of wood with the name *Smith* on it.

"Will you make something for me?" I'd finished my wine and my head was heavy, my words slow, but I gave Jake my best puppy-dog eyes and batted my lashes.

He chuckled; a sleepy twinkle in his eyes. "What do you want?"

"That's a very loaded question, Professor," I whispered and stepped closer.

"What would you like me to carve for you?" Jake amended.

I pursed my lips. "I'd like you to make something for me from your heart. Something you know I'd like. Something that just screams *Keegan*." I grinned broadly. "Maybe like a dildo or something."

Jake threw his head back and laughed. "I'm not sure hand-carved dildos are ever going to be my specialty. Not sure I'd want to get into the specifics for safe finishes and the ability to keep the piece properly sanitized."

"Well then, you think of something. It can be little, but I want it to be a surprise." I walked to the couch and sat down. "I wonder just how one would go about making a useable, washable wooden dildo," I mused.

Jake chuckled and joined me on the couch. "I'll leave it to others to figure out."

I stretched my bare feet out over his lap. At first, Jake just stared at my feet as if aliens had landed on his legs, but he eventually smirked, shook his head, and let his hands drape over my ankles. "Guess we'll sleep well tonight. Probably should have split today's work into two or three days. But I'm glad it's done."

"So exhausted," I mumbled with my head thrown back on the arm of the couch. "Like, my muscles are so limp and tired, I could probably take a big ol' cock with no prep at all. Just slide right in," I murmured sleepily. Clearly the wine had loosened my lips.

Jake coughed. "Jesus, Keegan. You can't say stuff like that. I'm an old man. I could have a heart attack."

I smiled with my eyes closed. "I'm kidding. My ass would still be nice and tight for any cock that wanted to fuck me. Know anyone looking?"

Jake groaned.

"Do you ever use toys? Like sex toys?" I asked.

"Um, no? I've never used anything on myself. I guess one woman did use a vibrator during sex, but she used it not me." He shifted under my legs.

Was he uncomfortable because he was disgusted or

turned on? If the bulge against my calf was any indication, I'd say he definitely wasn't disgusted.

"Toys are fun. With anal, you usually need to do some stretching and prep. Well, I mean, the prep is a must. Gotta clear the corridor so to speak," I teased. "But most bottoms don't *love* a dry dick shoved in an unprepped hole. Don't get me wrong, there's a time and a place, but a little stretching and lube isn't a bad idea most of the time. Or at least some spit," I rambled on sleepily. "Toys are two-fold because they are fun *and* they help with prep. Love wearing a butt plug—I mean, it's not like I've got any real-life guys lined up to fuck me, but I still love the full, stretched feeling. And it's good to work the plug out slowly and then slide a dildo in." I cracked an eye and saw Jake's head was thrown back against the couch and he was breathing deeply, his nostrils flaring. "Can you imagine how pretty a hand-carved wooden dildo would be?" I kept on pushing, knowing I was getting to him. "Just by itself it would be beautiful. But watching it slide in and out of an ass? God, so good."

"You. Are. Killing. Me," Jake bit out between gritted teeth.

I smiled. "It's okay to think about it. Think about sliding that gorgeous wood into my waiting hole before removing it to press your cock deep inside."

"Jesus Christ, Keegan." Jake shot off the couch. "Stop. It's too much."

"You're fun to tease," I said as I stood and wrapped my arms around his neck. "Nighttime hug."

Jake was tense, but he eventually loosened up and pulled me close. I sighed and melted into his warm strength.

I wanted to drop to my knees and worship the cock tenting his pants, but I decided I'd given Jake enough to think about for the night, so I just rocked my hips gently against him so he could tell I was as turned on as he was.

"Sorry," he mumbled as he pulled his hips away from me. "I guess your words really got to me."

I cupped his face. "Jake, there's nothing wrong with being turned on right now. It's okay to be questioning or bisexual or gay or pansexual or...well, the list goes on and on. You may be fantasizing about sex with men..."

"Not *men*. Man," Jake answered harshly. "A man I can't have. Keegan, I can't cross that line with you."

"Jake, there's no line to cross. I won't push you into something you don't want to do. Ever. But I need you to know that I'm wildly attracted to you. I'm not a child. My dad doesn't control my life—I honestly don't know how he'd react to finding out there was something between us. Really though, who's to say whatever is here would last more than a couple times?" I hated the thought of that, but I didn't want Jake thinking I was expecting a ring on my finger when he was clearly feeling jumbled about his sexuality in the first place.

Jake stepped closer again and took my face in his hands. "What I'm feeling is more than just sexual. I'm a fucked up headcase right now. Past attractions to men are haunting me despite years of pushing them aside. Wanting to experience every single thing you could show me has me in a perpetually turned-on, curious state. Thinking of our bodies together keeps me up at night." He rested his forehead against mine. "But it's more than that. It's wanting to take care of you. It's the desire to see you happy and safe. It's the thrill I get from making you laugh. It's the crazy thoughts I have about never wanting to let you go. Those are what run on a constant loop in my head—and I have no fucking clue where all of that has come from." He closed his eyes and breathed out slowly. "I know I'd just be a fun time for you. You're young and I'm sure you're not looking to settle down—especially with an old man. I want..." He huffed. "I want what you're teasing about, but I think I want more than that and it's not fair of me to expect that or put either of us through what would likely get emotionally messy."

My eyes stung with tears. "Jake," I whispered. My heart clutching in my chest.

"No." He held up a hand. "We're both exhausted and we drank too much wine. I can't sleep with my best friend's son. Partly because I don't want to ruin my friendship with Doc. Mostly because I'm not sure my heart would ever recover." Jake closed his eyes and shook his head. "If I thought we could just fuck a few times and be over it, I'd be completely on board with it. But come to find out, I'm a closet romantic and what I feel for you is—well, it's fucking crazy is what it is —but it's also a lot more than a few fucks. It's better if we are just friends and keep the sex and heart shit out of it."

I nuzzled my nose against his neck. "What if I told you that I feel that same *more* that you're feeling? What if I said I wanted all of the things you're talking about?"

He moved me away with strong arms. "I'd say we're tired, we're buzzed, and we need to go to bed. I can't be the man you need me to be."

I blinked and a hot tear ran down my face. "You already are," I whispered.

SEVEN

JAKE

I GROANED as I woke in my bed the next morning. My head throbbed from a bit too much wine and not enough water before sleep. My muscles screamed in protest of every movement—I'd overdone it the day before with all the garden work. My cock was painfully hard and I would have been lying to myself if I tried to say it was just morning wood.

Fucking Keegan.

When had any person had such an effect on me? The attraction steamrolled me and definitely had me in a perpetual state of horny confusion. But it was so much more. Without even trying, Keegan had somehow become this huge part of me. I couldn't stop thinking of ways to make him happy, keep him safe, make him smile. If he asked me to go replant the entire garden right that second, I'd drag my sore body out of bed and do just that. I couldn't say no to the kid.

You said no to him last night and he was upset.

Well, I'd said no to him last night because we weren't in the right headspace. He was young and horny and probably just wanted to fulfill some kink by getting his rocks off with an old man. If I already felt as strongly about Keegan as I did, what would that feeling be like once the intimacy of sex had been added to the equation? Maybe I was lonely. Maybe I desperately craved that physical connection. But there was no maybe about it, my heart would *not* survive loving Keegan and then losing him.

And Doc. Oh my God, Doc. What the hell would he think? He was open minded—about himself and others. About his best friend fucking his child? I truly had no idea how Doc would react.

Weird how you've never been able to say no to Doc and now you're feeling the same about his son.

Holy fuck.

I ran a hand through my hair and whimpered—even that movement hurt.

I closed my eyes and immediately my mind filled with Keegan. In that damn silk robe. It wasn't that I *wanted* him to cover up completely. I wanted him to be comfortable around me—this was his home. But the silk was driving me to distraction. Many times, he had a cotton tank and short— very short—shorts on underneath. Sometimes I'd catch glimpses of his smooth chest and soft pink nipples, or the curve of his butt cheek cupped by silk or lace panties as he stretched up to reach something from a high cabinet, and sometimes even the little splotch of darker skin right at the apex of Keegan's thigh and groin—a birthmark I assumed. Those were the times I wanted to toss myself into an ice-cold river just to ease the throbbing of my cock.

The Keegan in my imagination threw a smile over his shoulder and walked to the kitchen table. We'd fallen into a much-loved habit of eating meals together and I was so screwed—I'd never realized I was lonely, never realized I wanted someone to eat with.

Were you truly that oblivious to not realize you wanted companionship? Or were you settled and content until Keegan came along? Were you longing for company? Or is it just Keegan that you long for and can't imagine not having around?

I huffed at my subconscious thoughts. Maybe I'd been lonely before, but more than anything, my feelings now all had to do with Keegan. I couldn't imagine I'd have felt the same if some other person had needed a spare room to sleep in.

Trying to wrap my head around how I felt about Keegan was exhausting, overwhelming, and had me feeling off kilter. I'd never felt for *anyone* the way I felt about him. Hell, there were two women in my past who had sworn their undying love for me and begged for us to get married. Where were my feelings about loving and protecting and making someone smile *then*? I was less than interested. In the sex and in the relationship. Yeah, sex with women had always been fine. But nothing about those intimate relationships had ever turned me on even an iota as much as Keegan's sex talk did. And that was just *words*. But even if I pushed aside how crazy the insinuated sex made me, there were so many other things that had me fucked up about the kid. Had any hug in my entire life ever felt as good and right as holding Keegan in my arms? And even his fucking feet threw me for a loop—like, I would have rubbed them for him if that was what he wanted.

If, for even a moment, I let myself imagine my picture-perfect future, it would consist of Keegan moving in permanently. He could do his trauma informed care work—which I'd recently wondered about the feasibility of him doing that face-to-face or if a virtual approach would be better—and work toward his counseling license. We'd share our lives, our meals, our bed. He already fit into my tiny corner of the world so perfectly, and I wanted him to be there forever.

But it would be unfair of me to expect Keegan to settle—to even *want* to settle down—with a man my age. I wouldn't put him through the potential tension with Doc. I wouldn't put him through the very probable issue of me having health problems—or even just the normal issues that arose with age —while he was still young and vivacious. I *maybe* had another ten years of being able to keep up with him sexually and physically.

Jesus, Jake. You're in perfect health—as indicated by your yearly physicals. It's not like your dick is gonna shrivel up and fall off when you hit fifty.

Yeah, well. It still wasn't fair to Keegan.

What if Keegan would like to decide what's fair to him?

I sighed. Fine, I was being selfish. I knew there was no way I could touch him, be inside him, love him, and then have to let him go. My heart already hurt to think of him leaving; I couldn't get involved more than I already was.

How are you going to continually turn down his advances and stop your heart from falling even deeper?

"Lots of jerking off and cold showers," I groaned to myself and palmed my erection.

Rolling out of bed—every single muscle in my body cried —I padded to the bathroom, turned on the shower, undressed, and climbed into the blessed heat. I needed to get rid of my boner, get some coffee, and confirm the landscapers were coming. I'd lucked out when I'd called them the day before and they'd had a cancelation and could fit me in.

As the hot water cascaded down, I closed my eyes and imagined holding Keegan. Imagined his soft lips against my neck, our hard cocks rubbing together, and his fingers teasing my nipples. As much as I wanted to see Keegan's mouth on my cock, I was just as interested in tasting him, teasing him with my tongue, and bringing him to orgasm—I had a feeling watching Keegan come would be spectacular. As I fantasized, the Keegan in my head dropped to his knees. With his big blue eyes locked on mine, he gripped my dick and rubbed the head against his lips. Then his tongue teased my slit before he opened his mouth and took my length deep.

I stroked myself as I imagined gazing down to watch Keegan's pretty pink lips stretch around my cock. I cupped my balls and pressed a finger against my taint before venturing farther and playing with my hole. My tight balls tingled and I thrust my dick faster into my slick hand. With an image of Keegan's tongue teasing my hole, I threw my head back and came with a roar.

My shaky knees and heavy breathing made it interesting trying to finish my shower—I should have washed everything *before* jacking off to the hardest orgasm of my life. At least the movement and hot water had loosened my muscles slightly. Maybe with some coffee and ibuprofen I'd be able to function the rest of the day.

KEEGAN and I ate our breakfast on the patio and watched as the landscape crew pulled up and unloaded. An older man and three younger men walked toward the patio.

"Mr. Oakley?"

I stood and shook the man's hand. "Call me Jake."

"I'm Chad Lawson with Lawson's Landscaping. Glad we could fit you in. We should be able to have you finished up here in about four hours." Chad gestured toward the other three men, all much younger than him. "This is my son, Keith, and his two friends, Patrick and Trevor; they're working with me this summer for college money, but they're skilled and hard workers."

"Good to meet you all," I answered. "This is Keegan. We'll be in and around while you're working. Holler if you need anything. Thanks for coming so quickly; I'll be glad to have it done." I noticed that Keith gave me a quick glance, but mostly kept stealing looks at Keegan. *Believe me kid, I get it.* But Keith checking out Keegan gave me a bit of a start and a not-so-great feeling rumbling in my gut.

Holy shit. Was I jealous?

As the crew headed to their trucks, I caught Keegan's eye. "So, they were cute. Yeah? Hell, I don't know."

Keegan laughed. "Being bi or gay or whatever doesn't mean you're automatically attracted to every single person. I didn't really find any of them super attractive, but I'm sure they're nice enough guys."

"The son was checking you out," I stated and realized it almost sounded like an accusation.

Keegan just smirked and winked. "I'd check me out, too. I'm hot." He leaned over to whisper. "But I have my eyes on this sexy professor. No young landscaper for me."

"But if he wanted to hook up or something?" I prodded.

Keegan shivered a bit. "To be honest, he kinda creeped me out with the staring. I wasn't reciprocating, so it was a bit tense and uncomfortable." He shrugged. "Plus, I don't have the best track record with in-person hook-ups, so I'd likely need to know him for a while before trying that. *And*, I'm not kidding when I say I've only got eyes for one person right now." He paused and cocked his head. "My fantasies may involve a lot of kink and maybe multiple people, but relationship-wise, I'm a one-man type of guy."

I swallowed thickly. Did I want to hear about his fantasies? Yes. No. Fuck no, I didn't need to hear about them. Was my stomach doing all kinds of crazy things as I thought about Keegan being interested in a monogamous relationship with me? Yes. Fuck yes. But still no. None of the reasons I had listed to myself that morning had changed. There were too many lines to cross and I didn't want to fuck things up with Keegan or with Doc. Or with my damn sappy, romantic heart.

What if crossing those lines brought you and Keegan both the happiness and fulfillment you deserve?

And ruined my friendship with Doc?

Maybe. But what type of friend doesn't want to see you happy? And maybe it brings you closer than ever before as you share a love for Keegan.

I poured myself more coffee from the coffee carafe before picking up the newly purchased hot chocolate carafe I'd bought specifically for Keegan's drink preference.

He smiled up at me. "Thank you," he whispered. "I love that you thought of me and my precious hot chocolate. It's great being able to have more than one cup at a time."

I chuckled and winked. "Anything for you. Somehow, even though you didn't even ask, I can't say no to you. Figured you'd enjoy it." I shrugged.

Keegan widened his eyes as if to say *Really, you can't say no to me? I seem to recall you saying no to me last night.* But he just twisted his lips into a tiny smirk and shrugged. "I love it. And I promise to use your inability to say no to me for *mostly* good."

"Yeah? Something tells me our definitions of *good* may differ quite a bit," I grumbled.

"Does your definition of good include me on my knees, choking on your cock?" Keegan batted his lashes and bit back a smile.

I closed my eyes, gritted my teeth, and pushed the image away. "I'm going to ignore that."

"Party pooper," Keegan teased and then stuck out his tongue.

His very pink tongue. A tongue I wanted to taste. Wanted to suck on. Wanted to feel all over my body.

Holy fuck. I took a sip of my coffee and nearly burned my tongue off. Good. That was good. The pain would distract me.

Keegan stood up, pulled his silk robe around his short shorts and tank, and headed to the side of the house. "I'm going to check on my garden. I've got homework. I'll see you at lunch?"

I nodded and bit my tongue in a desperate attempt to stop thinking about Keegan's gorgeous ass.

AFTER LUNCH, Keegan begged off to go finish a paper he had to turn in, and I wandered to my studio. I wanted to make something for Keegan, but I wasn't sure just what. I loved that he'd been so interested in my hobby, but him requesting "the perfect piece" was giving me anxiety.

I closed my eyes and thought about Keegan. A history of trauma haunted him, but he was working through it between past therapy and current education and training. He also loved to dance, do makeup, and decorate his fairy garden. While those things weren't *all* that made up Keegan, they were things that stood out to me.

Suddenly, three ideas hit.

I'd make a sectioned organizer where he could keep his makeup and brushes and whatnot. I'd carve several little toadstools for his garden and maybe even a tiny table. And a worry stone. Something he could keep in his pocket and rub when he was feeling anxious.

I smiled. Suddenly, I adored the three ideas and wasn't sure which I wanted to start first. I opted for the worry stone because it would be the quickest. Then I'd do the garden decorations and the organizer.

I set to work finding the perfect piece of wood for the worry stone. Putting aside several pieces that would be great for making worry stones to sell online, I finally opted for a chunk of wood I knew would be gorgeous when finished.

An hour later, I was finished with the shaping and sanding and only needed to add a light sealer—I wanted the piece protected but not heavily lacquered.

As I drew sketches of toadstools and organizers, I couldn't help but think about Keegan's interest in wooden dildos. Once finished with my planning, I grabbed my studio laptop and searched for wooden dildos. As expected, they definitely existed. I perused several articles discussing the importance of shape, size, proper finishing, and ability to withstand moisture and sanitization—all which sealed my decision to leave the creation of these pieces to others with a lot more experience and skill than me. When I found a site with some of the most gorgeous wooden dildos I could have ever imagined, I browsed for several minutes before adding a butt plug to my cart. What the heck, I thought to myself, and added their best-selling dildo to the cart as well.

Three hundred fifty dollars later, I shook my head at the impulse purchases—Keegan wasn't wrong about being able to make bank selling hand-carved sex toys. But between the skill, time, and materials needed to make the items visually and physically appealing along with usable, a pretty penny was definitely understandable.

What the ever-loving hell was I going to do with a wooden butt plug and dildo?

Really? You're going to play like you don't know exactly what you want to do with your new toys?

I grumbled to myself. Fine. I definitely had ideas about ideal ways to use the purchases, but that didn't mean I'd ever *actually* allow it. Maybe one day—on a particularly rough day after Keegan had to leave—maybe I'd experiment with the pieces on myself. I sighed. I was stupid to buy them. They'd be useless to me. Maybe I'd give them to Keegan as a going away present.

What would it feel like to know Keegan wore that plug for

me? He said he loved the stretch and fullness. I closed my eyes and sighed as I pictured sliding the beautiful wood-grain dildo into Keegan's ass.

Imagining Keegan on my bed, legs spread, as he fucked himself on the wooden toy nearly brought me to my knees.

Fuck. I palmed my dick and breathed deeply. Keegan had me hard more often these days than I'd ever been in the prior thirty years. I thought of tomato worms, picking green beans in the sickening hot sun, grading a terrible essay, *anything* that would ease my throbbing dick.

After shutting down the laptop, I checked that the worry stone was drying correctly before organizing my sketches for the next two projects. Then I turned off the lights and left my studio.

I heard Keegan's voice and smiled. I walked to where he was sitting in the living room and paused as I realized he was talking on the phone.

Duh, you dumbass. What else would he have been doing? Just sitting in the living room having a conversation with himself?

"Yeah, I love it here. It's secluded but Jake and I can get anything we need. We even went to town to a little garden shop. I built a fairy garden and helped Jake plant a vegetable garden." Keegan sat curled in the corner of the couch, his back to me with me listening in like a damn stalker. "No, he's great. You were right. We get along really well. Except for living with you, I've never felt as comfortable to just be me, just be true to myself, as I do here," Keegan's voice cracked a bit—he was clearly talking to Doc. "Yeah, call again when you can. Mmhm, love you too." Keegan disconnected and sat there quietly for a moment.

Without a second thought, I walked to where he was sitting and placed a hand on his shoulder.

Keegan started and looked up to me with wide eyes—his face was level with my zipper.

"Sorry, I really didn't mean to eavesdrop," I mumbled.

He smiled. "It's okay. Dad called."

I nodded. "I want you to know that you can *always* be yourself. This is a safe place. And if we're ever out in public, don't ever worry about being yourself around me. I will never *not* want you to be you—to just be Keegan. And if you ever don't feel safe being *you*, just tell me and we'll go where we *can* be ourselves."

Keegan's eyes welled with tears. "Thank you," he whispered gruffly.

We stared at each other for what seemed like an hour before Keegan bit his lip and leaned over the arm of the couch to nuzzle his nose against my dick. "You change your mind yet?"

I allowed myself to enjoy Keegan's warm breath against my shorts for two seconds before swallowing thickly. "You want dinner? Maybe we make our own pizzas?"

A flash of something close to disappointment crossed Keegan's face, but he covered it with a smile. "Pizza and wine? Perfect." He winked and held his hand out to me.

The electricity that jolted through my body as I took his hand in mine was like a lightning bolt to my heart. I pulled him from the couch and caught him in my arms as Keegan wrapped his arms around my neck.

"Daily hugs," Keegan reminded me.

We stood in the quiet, warm embrace for several moments.

"The only thing that would make this hug therapy better would be if you'd kiss me," he murmured against my neck.

I closed my eyes and held him tight, his slim body fitting against me like a puzzle piece I'd never known I'd been missing in my life. "If I started, I may never stop," I whispered against the top of his head. "Best if we don't tempt fate."

"Or we welcome fate with open arms and enjoy what we both can tell would be amazing," Keegan shot back before pursing his lips and glaring at me with fiery eyes. "Jake, I get that you're scared. I get that this is all new to you. I get that you don't want to mess things up—with Doc, with me, with *whatever* it is you think may get messed up." He placed a hand on my chest. "But there's absolutely no way you can deny the heat between us. There's a connection. Something deeper than just sex. I can be patient—but I can also be persistent—I'm not ready to give up. I'm not a love 'em and leave 'em type guy. I don't want a quick fuck—okay, I *do*, but not *only* that—I want a relationship—which is crazy because I've never met anyone I wanted a real relationship with. Hell, who am I kidding? We already *have* a real relationship. I just want to take it to the next level." He stepped closer, adding his other hand to my chest and moving his hands up to cup my face. "I want to show you how amazing we could be."

I closed my eyes and leaned my forehead against Keegan's. "You're killing me. I can't just experiment with you. I can't betray your dad that way. And I can't suffer the heartache when you inevitably have to leave."

Keegan stepped back and crossed his arms over this chest. "That's a load of bullshit and you know it. Experimenting together could be the most amazing thing ever; we could both learn from each other. I love my dad, but he's not my keeper. I'm a grown man. I really don't know that he'd be angry—especially if we explain we have real feelings for each other—but either way, I don't have to answer to Doc and neither do you." His face softened, "I'm not inviting myself to stay here forever, but I need you to understand that I don't have any huge plans of where I'm going when I'm done with school. So, me leaving isn't a guarantee. Maybe we try this and you decide it's not for you and you end up *glad* that I'm leaving. If not, if you want me to stay, then I can stay. The

beauty of my career choice is that I can do it from anywhere
—even online which is what I've been planning on." Keegan
smiled slightly. "Please don't deprive us both of something
that could be the best thing that ever happened to us just
because of ridiculous reasons and fear."

"So, I'm ridiculous for being scared?" I bit out.

He shook his head. "No. Not at all. You're completely
normal to be scared. But feeding that fear with exaggerated
or invalid reasons isn't doing anything for your head or your
heart."

I sighed. "Let's just make pizzas, drink wine, and enjoy
our evening." I raised my brow and waited for Keegan's
reaction.

He huffed. "Fine. I love any time I get to spend with you."
He wrapped his arm around my waist and snuggled close as I
put my arm around his shoulders. "But don't expect me to
just give up on this."

"I wouldn't dream of it," I deadpanned.

Keegan giggled and bumped his hip against mine.

"OH MY GOD, I'm so full," Keegan wailed as he flopped next
to me on the couch. "Ohhhh, and I'm also *very* buzzed. The
room is spinning." He giggled.

"Well, we had wine as an appetizer, wine *with* our pizza,
and now we're working on the third bottle for dessert." I
smiled as his glassy eyes widened.

"You're right. We're a bunch of lushes. Good thing we ate
pizza to soak up some of the alcohol." A hiccup sent Keegan
into a fit of giggles.

"You liked your pizza though?"

"Mmmm, so good. I'll never be able to eat frozen or store-
bought again. I'm officially a homemade pizza slut." Keegan

crawled onto my lap, his back against the arm of the couch, his legs stretched across my thighs, feet on the cushion. And I was pretty sure I stopped breathing. "The homemade dough is the kicker. Don't get me wrong, the sauce was amazing, but the dough was the best part. I played it safe this time, but next time I want to try a white sauce, pesto, and a five-cheese blend." He burped softly. "Eeeww, but not now. I'm way too full." He drained the last drop of his wine and put the glass on the side table. "Was yours good?" Keegan turned toward me, propped against the couch arm, and placed a hand on my shoulder.

"Huh?" I asked, my brain still trying to cope with Keegan being draped across my lap.

"Was. Your. Pizza. Good?" Keegan tapped his finger on my collarbone.

"Oh, um, yeah. Even better when we can use tomatoes from the garden to make our sauce." My dick plumped behind my zipper because of Keegan on my lap while my heart fluttered at the thought of Keegan and me having our own pizza nights with homemade dough and sauce. Maybe even a date night from time to time. Would Keegan ever want to go out in public with me?

"Let's do real talk," Keegan quipped. "We ask questions and have to answer honestly."

"How do you know the other person is being honest?"

Keegan pursed his lips. "I trust you not to lie to me."

It took every ounce of strength I had not to wrap my hand around his neck and pull him close for a kiss. What would those pretty pink lips taste like? I wanted to feel his tongue against mine. Instead, I nodded.

"Tell me about the best sex you've ever had," Keegan commanded.

When I stared at him with my mouth gaping open for way too long, Keegan continued. "Fine, I'll go first. The best sex

I've ever had has always been with myself. The few physical encounters I've had were clumsy and inexperienced *or* rough and not *completely* consensual." Keegan frowned.

My heart caught and I took his hand.

"That's why I need you to trust me that I'll never ask you to do anything with me that you're not completely onboard with." Keegan squeezed my hand. "Sex with myself is great because I know exactly what I like." He shrugged. "Not going to say I don't wish I had a warm body to share it with. Okay, your turn."

I sighed. "Sex in the past has always just been okay. Nothing spectacular. The women I slept with were very nice and I likely could have made a very nice life with one of them." I shrugged. "But something was always missing— honestly, I thought something was wrong with me."

"Have you ever thought of sex with a man?" Keegan murmured, his thumb tracing along my knuckle. The kid was damn persistent and slowly but surely wearing me down.

He was right. I wouldn't lie to him. "Not before you. I convinced myself that all of the men I found attractive were for reasons other than physical or sexual, and I pushed the feelings away. It was fairly easy to do after a while and eventually I convinced myself that none of those past attractions even existed." I shook my head. "Then you came along and it all came pouring back in."

"But what's different this time? Why push it away back then but let it in and at least think about it now?" Keegan prodded.

I frowned and took a moment to consider the question. "I guess back then I was a lot more worried about my reputation, my career, my future. Now? Now none of that seems as important. I like my job, but I don't *need* it. My reputation is one of a lonely, anti-social hermit so there's not much to save or ruin there. My future? It didn't seem one way or another before, so I don't think being attracted to guys is going to mess that up." I took a deep breath. "I guess I've learned a lot about myself the older I've gotten. I want others to be able to be themselves around me—want to help others celebrate who they really are—so maybe I'm beginning to see it's okay for me to let down the walls and be a little more myself."

"But not with me?" Keegan whispered.

I ignored the clench of my heart. "My turn. You're always alluding to kinky fantasies. Tell me some of them."

Keegan narrowed his eyes. "I'll take the bait. For now." He shifted on my lap. "So, you know I love to dance and wear silk and lace. You know I love makeup. One thing you don't know is that I love to be watched while I dance and touch myself. Love knowing that others are getting off watching me jack myself or finger my hole. The thought of *you* watching me fuck myself on a big dildo is almost as much of a turn on as imagining how great your cock in my ass would feel." Keegan leaned closer, his forehead against mine. "I get off thinking about how I want to suck you, rim your ass, bend over for you. I come all over my hand and stomach when I imagine you thrusting your long, hard cock into my tight hole."

With no thought at all to the reasons I shouldn't, I closed the distance between us and touched my mouth to Keegan's. He gasped and any hope I'd had of the real thing not living up to my fantasies flew out the window.

Keegan pulled back just a smidge, licked his lips, his blue eyes questioning.

I wrapped my hand around the back of his head and pulled him close, my mouth devouring his. Keegan tasted of pizza and wine, but also of hope, fulfillment, and everything *right* that I'd recently realized I'd been missing.

He whimpered and opened his mouth, his tongue flicking

out to tease mine in the briefest of invitations. I dipped my tongue into his mouth and savored his sweetness for a moment before my balls drew up tight and I knew I had let things go too far.

I jerked back, maneuvered myself out from under Keegan's legs, and stood up breathing hard.

"Jake?" Keegan stared up at me, pink, puffy lips and big blue eyes.

I wiped the back of my hand over my mouth and shook my head. "I'm sorry, Keegan. That was completely inappropriate. We've both had *way* too much to drink and I lost control. I'm so very sorry." I turned and headed toward my office.

"Jake? Damn it, Jake!" Keegan called after me. "I'm maybe not one hundred percent sober, but I'm not drunk. I wanted that as much as you did. Jake?"

I closed the door behind me, locked it, and threw myself into the recliner. "You damn fucking fool. Show a little self-control." My head and heart throbbed as I battled over whether I was angrier at the kiss or angrier at how turned on I was. Or maybe I was angriest at the fact that I'd gone against my promises *and* I'd hurt Keegan in the process.

My cock ached, hard and leaving a definite wet spot behind my zipper. Knowing I couldn't have Keegan, no matter how badly I wanted him—or even how much he swore it was okay—I yanked my laptop from the coffee table onto my lap and did something I'd never allowed myself to do. If the FBI or other government agencies were truly spying on the general public, my agent was getting an eye full for the first time. First wooden dildos and now porn. Specifically, porn with the keywords *gay*, *silk*, and *lace*. Once I found a few videos, I began clicking the other keywords like *twink* and *femboy*. One channel I came across had a free preview from one of their top webcam performers—a video that had been posted within the last few weeks and already had thousands of views. *SilkNLace22* danced onto the screen. As I ogled his bare chest, pink nipples, and smooth stomach, I pushed the waistband of my shorts down and took my throbbing dick in my fist. I began to stroke as the performer turned around and teased the camera with his silk-clad ass. Then he swayed his hips and began to shimmy the material down over his perfect bubble-butt.

I gripped my dick and jerked hard.

When the man on the screen turned around, his perfect dick stood proudly from a trimmed thatch of dark blonde hair. He fisted his cock and thumbed his slit to spread his precum.

Words popped up on the screen. *Want to watch more? Subscribe now! Subscribers can gain access to private webcam performances. Tell SilkNLace22 what you want and he'll make your wildest dreams come true.*

Just as my balls drew up tight and an orgasm shattered through me, my brain registered two things there was *no way* I could ignore. *SilkNLace22* slowly pulled his silk panties up and over his still-hard cock, but not before I saw a splotch of darker skin right at the apex of his thigh and groin. And then he pulled on a fucking purple silk robe.

With my spent dick still in hand, I searched my brain to make sense of what I'd just seen. I went back a bit in the video and studied the background. It was dark, but I was able to see the white comforter on the bed behind him. A white comforter just like the one in Keegan's room.

Anyone could have a white comforter.

A birthmark, a purple robe, and a white comforter? That was way too much coincidence. I was ninety-nine-point nine percent sure that *SilkNLace22* was Keegan. Fuck, even the screenname fit.

I quickly cleared my history, wiped up my mess, and made

a beeline for my bedroom. After a shower, I fell into bed a mass of confusion and worry.

I felt ashamed that I'd jacked off to Keegan's video. Was what he was doing even safe? Was Keegan in a bad situation? And fucking hell, why did I want to watch and re-watch every second of that video?

THREE DAYS LATER, I was still thinking about the whole damn situation. I wanted to watch it again. I wanted to watch all of Keegan's videos. But I also worried about Keegan's safety. Would he tell me about it if I asked? Keegan had been pretty snippy with me since the kiss—he didn't seem to be in the talkative, sharing mood.

Maybe I'd just keep it quiet. Not let him know that I knew about his webcam channel. I'd just keep him safe. How? Fuck if I knew, but I had to. Yeah, I'd keep an eye on him, let him continue doing what he was doing, and never tell him I'd accidentally found his video and jacked off to it.

I made it exactly one day from the moment I made that decision. After Keegan had been quiet at dinner, I shut myself in my office and gave in to my damn stupid curiosities. Let's be honest, I was horny and nosy. And I was butt-hurt that Keegan was mad at me—it hurt that he didn't understand I was trying to protect him.

Again, maybe you should let Keegan decide what he wants and what he may or may not need protecting from.

Ignoring the thought, I opened my laptop. I found the site, paid for a subscription, and found his channel. With an upgrade to my subscription, I became a super fan with access to private videos, chat, and live performances. Holy shit that was easy.

Before I could click on anything else, I slammed the laptop shut.

"What in the actual fuck are you doing, Oakley?" I muttered to myself. I didn't have an answer. Any reason I could give would just sound like an empty, pathetic excuse.

You've got the real man—the very real, very willing man—right down the fucking hallway. What do you need with his webcam channel?

"I don't know," I growled to the empty office.

"Shut your piehole," Bucko croaked.

I groaned.

"Fuck off," the bird added.

"Back at ya," I grumbled to Bucko.

When I should have immediately canceled my subscription and blocked the website, I simply put the laptop to the side. As I covered Bucko's cage, I promised myself I'd try to ignore the pull to watch Keegan's performances. It felt wrong and creepy. Not wrong that I'd watch something sexual. Not wrong that I'd get off watching a beautiful man. But that I'd sneak around and watch Keegan without his knowledge.

Wondering what those videos held was going to kill me. I'd started along a very slippery slope and I was losing my footing. Fast.

Maybe if I could fulfill my curiosities by watching Keegan's videos I'd be able to keep my hands off of the real Keegan.

And maybe you're a fucking idiot.

I sighed heavily and left the office.

Yeah, that was a definite possibility.

EIGHT

KEEGAN

"You've been weird," I accused Jake at dinner a few days after the kiss.

Jake looked up from his dinner like a deer in headlights. "Huh? Oh, um, just trying to give you space."

"I don't need space," I answered.

"You're mad at me." Jake shrugged. "I'm sorry for kissing you."

My fork clattered to the table a bit louder than I'd intended. "Stop apologizing for kissing me. And I'm not *mad*. I'm frustrated." I wiped my mouth and placed the napkin on the table. "Frustrated on several levels. One, I'm horny and I want you so badly every single cell of my body is on edge. Two, I'm frustrated that you won't accept there's something between us." When Jake started to protest, I held up my hand. "Fine, you've accepted there's something between us, but you won't allow it to happen. As half of the participating equation, I feel like I'm getting the raw end of the deal. Like *Jake* has decided. *Jake* is the older and wiser one. *Jake* knows best. Well, fuck that. Maybe I'm not your age, maybe I don't have your life experiences, but I'm intelligent and level-headed enough to know what I want. I want *you*. Am I being a pouty brat because you won't give me what I want? Yeah, probably. Which yes, I totally see the irony that I want to be treated like an adult and I'm acting like a child." I sipped my ice water. "Honestly? The thing that maybe has me the most frustrated is that you are starting to allow yourself to open up, maybe explore this attraction to men, accept that sexuality is fluid and you *may* be bisexual or even something else...and you don't want to allow me to be a part of any of that. On one hand, I'm thrilled you're allowing yourself to question and explore. But on the other hand, it hurts like hell that you maybe want sexual experiences with a man...just not *this* man." I stared down at my hands. "And I'm already scared of how much it will hurt when you have other men over while I'm still here."

Jake stood and walked to my side of the table. He dropped to his knees and took my hand. "Keegan, listen to me. That kiss was amazing. *You're* amazing. Yes, I'm learning a lot about myself and it feels good to let that knowledge in and just accept *me*. But I have no plans, thoughts, or desires to hook up with or explore with other men. Not at this point in time. My head isn't in the right place to even consider that." He squeezed my hand. "I swear to you. If I ever get to a point where I can push all of my doubts and concerns out of my head, I'll come to you. You are the only person I'd ever feel comfortable exploring with."

I smiled sadly. "I guess I'm just worried we'll miss out on something spectacular because you won't push back against those doubts and concerns. It's like you use them as a security blanket to protect yourself. And I get that, I do. But eventually, you have to allow a crack in that wall if you're ever going to grow past the questioning and accepting yourself stage. I don't want you to stay wrapped up, protected, and missing out on what we could be." I stood and pulled him to his feet so I could wrap my arms around his waist and tuck my head under his chin. "Have you ever had your balls and ass crack waxed?" I asked.

Jake's entire body shook with laughter. "Where the fuck did that come from?"

I lifted my chin and smiled up at him. "I have a point. Just answer the question."

He shook his head. "No, can't say that I have."

"Okay, that's alright. I actually would have been surprised if you said yes." I pushed him backwards until his hips hit the kitchen counter. "So, I would never be able to wax my own balls or ass crack. I'd get the wax on and just freeze with fear. The anxiety would be debilitating and I'd be left with wax stuck to my pubes and nothing to show for it except a huge oily mess as I tried to clean the wax off."

Jake raised a brow and smirked.

"Hang on, I'm getting there." I poked his chest. "But when I go to the salon and have a professional slather hot wax on my balls and crack, the anxiety is still there, but there's no freezing up because I don't have to control it. She yanks that shit off, I whimper a bit, and then it's done. Baby-butt-smooth balls and ass until the next appointment."

Jake narrowed his eyes. "I'm not following. First, why must you tease and give me that image? Second, while I get the wax scenario—I never would have thought you'd get waxed since that requires public contact—I'm not sure how ripping off hot wax from your balls has anything to do with our situation."

I giggled. "First, I *can* go out in public, I just often choose not to. Second, I did do waxing for a while, but got lasered a while back so I don't actually do the wax thing anymore. But the *point* is that I'm the professional so to speak. You're the guy with his legs spread and hot wax on his balls. If we waited for you to yank it off, we'd never get anywhere. But if you let me, I can have your balls and ass smooth in just a few quick rips."

"You really want to wax my balls?" Jake frowned.

I started then stopped then started again. "I mean, I'd totally do that if you wanted me to. Although I'm not at all opposed to you being all-natural."

"I mean, I trim and shit," Jake muttered.

I winked. "Good to know. But the *point* to this story—which admittedly got way off track—is that maybe you should hand over control and let me make decisions for a while. Like ripping off wax or riding a roller coaster or pulling the cord on a reverse bungee ride—all of those things are situations where you've given consent to participate and then the climactic parts are out of your hands. If you give me consent—agree to see what could possibly happen between us—then I can be the one yanking off the wax strip or pulling the cord. Sometimes it's easier to let others do it—the fear and anxiety can get in our own way and make us freeze up."

Now, if I'm being honest, I had *no fucking clue* where that whole speech came from. It wasn't on my mind until that exact moment—definitely hadn't rehearsed it or thought it through. But it wasn't half bad. Actually, it was pretty damn good.

Jake stared at me for a moment. "Just to clarify. If I agree to wanting something with you—kinda like spreading my ass cheeks for the wax or stepping into the roller coaster car—you'll make the moves, call the shots, get things started instead of me drowning in a pool of fear, uncertainty, and the unknown?"

"Exactly!" I crowed. "What do you say? Hand the reins over to me and let me drive?" I stepped closer and placed my hands on his chest. "I promise to do it right, make it good."

"I don't know that anything between us could ever be

anything but good," Jake murmured. "I think I like the idea. Maybe. But can we both think it over for a bit?"

I nodded. "Yeah, that's cool. I've got some work to do." Actually, I had several webcam performances scheduled, but those technically qualified as *work*, so I wasn't being completely untruthful. For a moment, I wondered if I should tell Jake about the webcam channel. Would it bother him? Would he judge me? I pushed away the thought. Jake had enough going on without needing to add in my kinky webcam side hustle. Besides, I wasn't planning to do that dancing and jerking off on camera forever. It was good money. The way it turned me on and got me off was an added bonus. But maybe if I ever got Jake in my bed, I'd have no more need for the webcam gig. "So, we'll talk at breakfast? See where we're at?"

Jake nodded. "Yeah, sounds good. I'll be working in my office for a while tonight."

I studied him. "You sure your weirdness has only been from that kiss? Because you seem extra weird. Like there's something you're not telling me."

Jake frowned and shook his head, but I didn't miss the blush. "No, just have my mind on work and other shit. Not doing a great job of compartmentalizing."

I wasn't completely sure he was telling me everything, but who was I to judge? I wasn't telling him *everything* either—it wasn't like I expected us to have zero secrets. Everyone had secrets. As long as our secrets didn't harm the other person, it was fine. Right? So why did I feel like we were both keeping something huge from each other? "Okay, well, get your work done."

Jake smiled and put a hand in his pocket. "Oh, I almost forgot. I made something for you." He pulled out a small wooden object and handed it to me.

I gasped and took the smooth little medallion of wood. "It's like a little worry stone," I exclaimed.

Jake smiled. "That was what I meant for it to be. Thought it would fit in a pocket and you could rub it if you were feeling worried or anxious."

"I love it. It's so perfect. Thank you." I threw my arms around his shoulders and melted into his heat as he squeezed me tightly. My eyes stung with tears. "Really, thank you. The fact that you know me well enough to understand why this piece is perfect for me, it means a lot. And I'll always be able to carry a little piece of you with me. Thank you." I kissed his cheek.

I walked to my room with a huge smile on my face. I wasn't one hundred percent sure the little speech I gave would work, but it made complete sense and Jake hadn't completely balked. I was more hopeful now than I had been before dinner. Maybe things were looking up.

I quickly showered and prepped myself. Then I set up the lighting, logged in under my screen name *SilkNLace22*—super original, I know—and looked to see what was scheduled. I had two live videos—one that would end before I came in hopes that the horny viewers would subscribe for more access. The other would be for the subscribers and they'd get the *happy ending* their monthly payment allowed.

There were also requests for private live videos. I didn't always take those. I wasn't under any obligation to do the private live ones. But I often checked through to see the requests. Usually they were creepy and made me feel uncomfortable, so I just deleted them. But there were sometimes requests that piqued my interest enough to make it worth my while.

The only ones I saw right then were creepy ones, so I deleted them all and focused on the two live performances I needed to do. Some viewers would watch live, but the scenes would be recorded and uploaded to my channel for later viewing as well. Maybe I'd check later and see if anyone *not creepy* had requested a private show.

I set the camera to record, linked to the site so viewers could watch live, and wrapped my robe around my waist. I'd give it a couple minutes to get a few viewers logged in before I started.

Knowing this first video would stop before the *good part*, I planned to make it as enticing as possible so the viewers would be begging for more. Then, of course, the link to the next video would pop up and their horniness would take over and they'd buy. Well, many would. It was the nature of the beast.

As I did during every show since moving into Jake's house, I imagined the eye of the camera was Jake as I started to touch myself. Knowing that the view started at my neck and only showed to my thighs, I got lost in the anonymity as I teased my nipples, ran fingers over my belly, and slowly pushed the robe from my shoulders. I imagined the audience —imagined *Jake*—pulling out his cock and groaning as he began to stroke himself. Standing up, I did the normal— almost required, always expected—slow turn to show off my perky ass cupped in silk before turning back around and shimmying the silk panties down inch-by-inch until my cock sprang free. I wasn't huge, but I had a nice, long dick that I felt wasn't too thick or too thin. When my fantasies traveled to Jake's fist on me, his mouth, his tongue, I knew I needed to get a few more parts packed into the scene before I shut it down—shut myself down at least for a moment or two. Hell, I still had to do the big ending and that would be difficult if I creamed myself just thinking about Jake. So, I thumbed my slit, stroked myself, cupped my balls, and whimpered. As my strokes got harder and faster, I reached to kill the camera—

leaving the viewers completely hanging. Then I stripped completely and headed to the bed.

Switching to slightly different lighting, a new camera position angled so they could see me from neck down, and getting a dildo and lube out of my drawer, I linked to the subscribers live feed and hit record. Still thinking of Jake, I jacked myself and moaned for a few moments before slicking my fingers with lube and teasing my hole. The image of Jake's tongue opening me, his fingers filling me, and his cock stretching me as he slid inside nearly had me coming before I got to the dildo. Holy shit, if the *thoughts* of Jake touching me had me so wound up, what would it be like if he ever actually touched me?

Picturing Jake reaching for the dildo, thinking of his eyes on me, I pressed the silicone head against my hole and panted at the inch-by-inch invasion. With the stinging stretch and fullness driving me, I slowly pumped the dildo in and out as I stroked my cock. When my balls drew up tight, I pressed the dildo deep and whimpered as my cock exploded all over my chest and stomach. Knowing the audience always loved to watch me slide the toy from my ass, I worked it out slowly before trailing a finger through the sticky mess on my belly. Then I moved to stop recording, wiped myself with a tissue, and lay still for a moment catching my breath. It was always good—orgasms had that effect on a body—but I longed to curl up and cuddle next to a warm, loving man after he'd brought me such pleasure.

Maybe one day. I sighed and rolled from the bed.

Before showering, I checked my private performance requests.

WoodyBoy: Can a private performance just be chatting?

. . .

I THOUGHT THROUGH THE QUESTION. Usually, private performances were for viewers to tell me what they wanted to see, but nothing said they couldn't be just to chat. I shrugged. If he wanted to pay extra just to chat, I was game.

SilkNLace22: Sure. Let me shower. Fifteen minutes?

WoodyBoy: I'll be here.

FIFTEEN MINUTES LATER, I fixed the camera on my laptop to see only from neck down and wrapped a black robe around my shoulders before messaging him the link to my live feed. I was glad this guy just wanted to talk because I wasn't sure I could get it up again if I tried.

The screen went dark and then I saw someone sitting in a dimly lit room with a plain wall behind him. The man wore a mask and was hidden mostly in shadows.

"Hi," I said in greeting. "So, what do you want to talk about?"

The man froze and then cleared his throat. "Honestly? I don't even know. I'm not sure I should even be on this site. But I couldn't stop myself."

I chuckled. "That's the way it goes usually."

"Do you feel safe doing what you do?"

"Safe? Yeah, almost completely. I mean, I guess someone could hack in and find me and then track me down, but mostly I feel safe." I'd thought about that a lot. Online like I did was a lot safer than turning tricks in real-life. And I never showed my face.

"And you like doing it?"

I shrugged. "The money is good. I get off knowing people

get off watching me. It's not a life-long commitment, but it's fun and lucrative for now."

"So being watched is a kink. What are your other kinks? Like things you've never told anyone?" A bird squawked in the background.

I narrowed my eyes. "Was that a bird?"

The man eased further back into the shadows. "Sorry, nature show on the television."

I pursed my lips. "Since we just met, why don't you tell me some of your fantasies first."

He was quiet for several moments. "I don't even know. I want my partner to trust me, to feel good, and to get off. That's about as far as I've ever let myself go."

"Spanking? Choking? Leather play? Piss play? Blindfolded? Tied up?"

He shook his head and almost gasped for air. "I...I really...I just don't know," he choked out. "I'm not against anything, I just haven't tried much. I just want my partner to be cared for."

Taking mercy on the guy, I smiled. "That's okay. Not everyone has a kinky side and not everyone with a kinky side finds it right out of the gate. Some people have kinks in a relationship they'd never have with random hook-ups. There's no real right or wrong when it comes to kink as long as it's safe and consensual." I pulled my legs up to my chest. "So, I'll tell you something I've never told anyone else."

Why was I willing to tell this guy my kinkiest kink? Maybe because he was a complete stranger who I'd never see again. Maybe because he seemed scared to admit anything he may want outside of *normal*. Maybe because my deepest desire had been bottled up for way too long. "My kinkiest fantasy involves me in a loving relationship—a strong and steady relationship—where my partner sets up a cum dump scene for me because he knows I want it. He lines up three to five willing men, takes me—blindfolded—to a secret location like a hotel room or similar. He sends me to the bathroom to prep myself. Then has me bend over the bed while he rims me. Soon, there's a knock on the door and I hear several male voices. He tells the men to strip. He reminds them all that they will wear a condom and when they are close to climax they are to pull out, take off the condom, and come all over my back."

Holy shit. I'd never voiced this out loud and it was totally turning me on.

The masked man grunted and shifted in his seat.

"My partner sits naked next to me on the bed—sometimes pushing his cock between my lips, sometimes just teasing me because he knows I want to suck him—and describes the cock of each man as the participants approach. He makes me tell him how each cock feels as it breaches my hole. As each man fucks me and comes on me, my partner pays them and tells them get dressed and leave. When we're alone, he wipes my cum-covered back clean and slides his bare cock deep into my well-used ass. He fucks me, telling me how much he loves me, and he doesn't pull out—he fills my ass with his hot, sticky cum. Then we sleep for a bit until he wakes me, rolls me to my back, slides his cock into my greedy hole, and makes love to me while he holds me and tells me how perfect I am and how much he loves me."

A tear rolled down my cheek.

The man put a hand to his mouth.

And a familiar voice croaked, "What's up, Bucko?"

I froze.

With panic and anger racing through my blood, I shot from my room and ran down the hall. Hot tears streamed down my face as I slammed into Jake's office. I kept hoping I was wrong. Jake was in bed or working quietly on his papers. Maybe I'd just heard Bucko through the wall.

But, no. There was Jake. His laptop open on his desk, a plain wall behind him, the mask beside him, as he rested his head on his arms, his shoulders shaking.

"What the fuck, Jake?!" I screamed.

"Keegan," Jake started, looking up with red eyes and a look of desperation, "I'm so, so sorry."

"I would have told you *all* of that. Every single word. *For free*. Instead, you sneak into my private chats and *pay me* like a fucking prostitute? Am I no better than a whore to you?"

"What? No!" Jake exclaimed.

"Well, congratulations on being the first person to *ever* make me feel dirty and disgusting." I slammed out of the office and rushed to my room.

An hour later, when the water had run cold and my tears were dried up, I climbed out of the shower and fell into bed. My heart ached. I wanted to talk to Jake, to hear him out, but it all hurt too much.

Maybe with some sleep, things would look different in the morning.

When I woke from way too few hours of sleep, my head was pounding from all of the crying.

And there were two hearts drawn in the condensation on my window.

I frowned. Drawing hearts didn't seem to be Jake's MO, but I also hadn't expected him to bomb my webcam channel and trick me into spilling my deepest secrets.

But you're not exactly turned off by the fact he was probably watching your videos. And you have to admit it's kinda hot that he now knows your kinky fantasy.

"Yeah, but I would have shown him that and shared all of that without him paying for a damn subscription. I'm right here," I whispered. "I'm right here."

NINE

JAKE

FUCK.

I'd never felt so miserable in my entire life. Guilt, shame, anger, humiliation, and fear all vied for attention in my head and heart. I didn't sleep a wink and I felt every minute of lost sleep as I dragged my pathetic ass to the kitchen. First, a double shot of espresso. Then a strong cup of coffee. If the caffeine hadn't put me out of my misery by then, I was going to speak to Keegan.

Last time I fucked up—yeah, it was beginning to be a pattern with me where he was concerned—I put off talking to him for too long. Not this time. I wasn't sure how I could make it right—or even *if* I could make it right—but I owed him an apology.

And an explanation?

But how could I explain something I didn't even understand myself?

Try, asshole.

Thirty minutes later, I felt somewhat alive thanks to the jumpstart shot I'd consumed. Hopefully the large mug would keep me going for a bit. When I heard the shower down the hall shut off, I waited about five minutes then stirred up a mug of hot chocolate and went to Keegan's door.

I knocked softly.

"What?" Keegan bit out. He was angry, but I also heard hurt.

"Can we talk? I owe you an apology."

He cracked the door, his wet hair artfully ruffled. "You do." Keegan eyed the mugs. "Is one of those for me?"

I held one cup up. "Hot chocolate."

Keegan narrowed his eyes and pursed his lips. "Fine. But not here. Living room is more neutral."

I nodded. "I'll meet you there."

Two minutes later, Keegan climbed into my lap, his back against the arm of the couch, his legs over my thighs. He stretched to reach the mug of hot chocolate on the coffee table. "I'm listening."

I took a deep breath. If Keegan was still willing to curl up with me, maybe I hadn't ruined things completely.

Ruined what things? You said there couldn't be anything between the two of you.

Yeah, well, maybe I was reconsidering after Keegan offered to lead the way.

"So, two things. First—and not *as* important as the apology, but still important—I thought about what you said. About you taking the lead. I don't think I'd realized how paralyzed with fear and uncertainty I was. I think having the decision-making part taken away from me—at least for a while, until I get over the initial worries—would be good for me. If you're still interested. I know I may have screwed up that offer completely."

Keegan eyed me over his mug. "Go on."

"I'm sorry about watching you." I frowned. "I'm not actually sorry about watching you. I'm sorry about not telling you. I'm sorry for sneaking and hiding. I didn't set out to find you."

Keegan frowned. "How *did* you find me?"

My cheeks heated. "I typed in *gay*, *lace*, *silk*, and *porn*. Then once I started finding things, I clicked the words *twink* and *femboy*."

He smirked and shrugged. "Well, the site will be glad to know their keywords are working." He raised his brows in a *go on* gesture.

"So, I found a preview video that ended up being you. But I didn't realize it was you at first." I felt like a little kid trying to explain my way out of a big time whuppin'.

"I don't show my face. *Ever*. How did you figure out it was me?"

"Your birthmark was what drove it home for me. Connecting that with the purple silk robe, *SilkNLace22* screen name, and white bedspread behind you gave me all the clues I needed."

"How do you know about my birthmark?" Keegan whispered.

I rolled my eyes. "You walk around scantily clad half the time—which by the way I love because it means you're comfortable around me, but I also hate because it keeps me fighting a raging hard-on at all times—so I've caught glimpses here and there."

Keegan licked his lips. "I kinda love knowing that you've been looking." But he sobered. "I'm still hurt and angry," he added.

"I know. And you have every right to be." I sipped my coffee. "So, when I should have closed my laptop and asked you about it, I made the mistake of thinking with my dick instead of my head. All I was going to do was subscribe. Just to...fuck, I don't even know what my plan was. But I wasn't going to watch. I don't even know how I convinced myself it was okay. Then I got concerned about your safety. When things were weird over the kiss…"

"*You* made that situation," Keegan interrupted.

"Yeah, I know. Anyway, my best laid plans to just ignore the site went out the window after you suggested the whole *Keegan Take the Wheel* scenario."

Keegan giggled. Then he frowned. "Keep going."

"I lost all control. I got to thinking about all the things I don't know. All the things I want to experience and learn. My curiosity got the best of me and I logged in. I swear I didn't know you were doing a live performance. But I was gone from the first moment I saw you. Hook, line, and sinker," I cleared my throat, "and I'm not just talking about the video."

Keegan's eyes shimmered.

"I'm clueless in most things sex-related. I mean, I can jack off with the best of them, and I'm pretty sure most of the women I slept with got off at least some of the time—hell, I don't know, maybe they were good fakers. But I'm a thousand percent clueless about anything sex-related with another man. I know what feels good to me, but I don't know what to *do* with another man." I ran a hand through my hair. "I can't say that I got on to watch you purely for research purposes. That would be a lie. But I do know that I wanted to learn something, *anything* that would maybe make me not so pathetic in bed."

Keegan cupped my face and kissed my cheek. "Never." He nuzzled his nose against my jaw.

"But then I wanted more. I wanted more than what others got to see. My head kept telling me to just go to you, talk to you, you're right here in my fucking house. Instead, like some type of damn creeper, I paid for a private performance. I'm so, so sorry. I violated your trust and I don't know how to make that right."

"I accept your apology. I think the part that hurts the

most is that you felt you had to lie and keep it like some dirty little secret. I'm not ashamed of what I do; it's liberating and empowering. But being paid by the only person I've ever felt such strong feelings for was like a slap in the face." Keegan's words were soft and sincere. "I'd like to think we can move on from this—if you're still willing—but I think it would be best if we take a bit of time apart. Emotions are high right now. Moving into something sexual at this point would be a terrible idea. Let's give ourselves a few days to think, to work through our feelings, and come back to it." He ran a hand along my cheek and brushed through the hair above my ear. "Is that okay?"

I nodded, my heart in my throat. "I'm good with that. It seems like a smart move. Just know that I'd made the decision to let you take the lead *before* I got caught like a fucking child with my hand in the proverbial cookie jar." I took his hand. "I don't want you thinking I'm giving in to your persistence just as a desperate attempt to get you to forgive me."

Keegan studied me for a moment and nodded. "I believe you." He leaned close. "Before we go our separate ways and spend some time apart to clear our heads, I have a favor to ask."

"Anything," I answered, shocked to hear how breathless my voice sounded.

"Kiss me," Keegan whispered.

My eyes locked on his and the world stopped spinning. Gently, I cupped a hand on his cheek and brushed my lips against his. Just a whisper of a touch. "Like that?"

"Oh, so the professor is a tease?" Keegan taunted. "I think you can do better."

I pulled him close and pressed my lips against his. Every other kiss in my entire life—all of them combined into one— didn't stand a chance against that one soft touch of Keegan's mouth against mine. If the heavens could have opened and shone down brilliant light while angels played their harps and trumpets, *that's* how the kiss felt.

Keegan made a little moaning sound against my lips and opened for me.

I teased his bottom lip before dipping my tongue in to dance with his. Keegan's chocolate flavor mixed with my coffee. I never wanted my lips anywhere but right there. Or maybe I could think of a few other places.

Keegan pulled back, breathless. "Okay, that has to suffice for now. We *really* need to clear our heads. Thank you for explaining. Thank you for the apology. I *do* think we can get past it. But we'd be making a mistake to jump into something so meaningful and important when we've just had such a disconcerting situation." He smiled softly. "At least *I* think it's meaningful and important."

I wrapped my arms around him and pulled him close. "There's never been something as meaningful and important —and scary and monumental—in all of my life. Do you still want to eat meals together?"

Keegan pulled back and cocked his head. "Let's play it by ear. If we're there to eat at the same time, fine. If not, just eat on our own?"

I swallowed the lump in my throat. "I kinda love our meal times. I miss you already."

Keegan nudged his nose against mine. "I kinda love our meal times too. You won't have to miss me for long. Promise." He placed a gentle kiss against my lips and crawled off my lap. "Thank you."

As I watched him walk away, I wondered at how close I'd come to ruining something special before it even had a chance to get started. For a younger person, Keegan was an absolutely amazing man with a huge heart. I had a feeling he was a lot smarter than me in *sooo* many ways. And I was man enough to admit that, step aside, and let Keegan lead the way while I learned.

I could only hope he still wanted that.

You planning on discussing that cum-dump fantasy with him?

I sighed and palmed my dick. "Yeah. Definitely. But not right now," I mumbled to myself.

You're totally thinking about a way to make it happen, aren't you?

"Don't be stupid. I've never even given a blow job, what in the hell would I know about setting up a cum-dump?" My words seemed to bounce around the empty room.

Where there's a will, there's a way. And we both know how much you enjoy making Keegan happy.

"Yeah," I sighed as if already giving into the fact that I'd likely do *anything* to see Keegan happy and smiling.

AFTER ONE DAY of comfortably existing in the house together, but not seeing much of each other, the second day seemed to be going mostly the same way. Keegan smiled at me as he made his evening hot chocolate. We chatted a tiny bit about our respective classes, how the garden was growing, and the landscaping.

"Hey, did the crew come back for anything?" Keegan asked.

"Not that I know of." I frowned. "Why?"

He shrugged. "I just thought I'd seen more work done. I should just take care of my fairy garden and not worry about the rest."

"Oh, I have some items for your garden." I headed toward my studio and smiled when I felt Keegan following. I picked up the five tiny toadstools I'd carved and handed them to him. "Toadstools for your fairies to sit on." I winked.

"Oh my God, they are so adorable. Thank you so much."

Keegan threw his arms around me and hugged me tight. "I'm going to put them in the garden right now while there's still light. Then I can enjoy them while I'm working." He turned to leave, but glanced over his shoulder. "I'll probably relax in my room most of the night after I finish homework. Breakfast date?"

I nodded with a smile. "See you then."

Several hours later, as I watched a documentary and nodded off while reading the same page over and over, I contemplated just going to bed. It wasn't *late* late, but I was tired. The sooner I went to bed, the sooner breakfast with Keegan would arrive.

A scream shattered the peaceful silence and I vaulted from the recliner with only one goal. Get to Keegan.

We met in the hallway and he threw himself into my arms.

"What's wrong? What happened?" I asked as I rubbed his back, my heart pounding a million times a minute.

Keegan took gulps of air as tears streamed down his face. "A man…a man was at my window…exposing himself…he was there, Jake, I swear. I'm not making it up. I'm not just being dramatic or hysterical."

"Hey, hey," I whispered and cupped his face. "Of course, you're not making it up."

Keegan swallowed and nodded. "My mom used to accuse me of just overreacting to things. Like when that guy got too rough with me? She said I was being dramatic and I should have been grateful anyone wanted me at all." He sniffed. "She died shortly after, so I know she wasn't in her right mind, but I'm always afraid people think I'm just being hysterical or overreacting."

"Never. I'll always believe you." I brushed a tear from his cheek and ground my molars thinking about how much I did *not* like his mother. Dead or not. "Now, can you tell me more about what happened?"

Keegan glanced around wildly. "Can we make sure all the doors and windows are locked and covered, please? I'm freaking out. It feels like he can still see me."

I held Keegan's hand as we walked from door to door and window to window making sure each was locked and covered. Then we sat on the couch. "Okay, tell me from the beginning."

Keegan frowned. "Well, I think it goes back a bit before tonight. After that night with the webcam, did you draw two hearts in the condensation on my window?"

My blood ran cold. Had someone been watching Keegan? I shook my head. "No. Why?"

"Well, it didn't seem like something you'd do, but I kinda forgot about it until now." He was quiet for a moment. "And remember I asked you about the landscaping crew? I saw muddy footprints on the little sidewalk outside my window. That's why I thought they'd come back to finish things." He gasped. "And I put the toadstools in the garden, did some homework, took a shower, and then looked out the window only to find that my garden had stuff roughed up, knocked over. At the time, I chalked it up to a squirrel or bunny, but..." He shuddered and curled against me.

"Okay, tell me more about what you saw."

Keegan took a deep breath and blew it out slowly. "So, I was irritated about the garden getting knocked over, but I didn't want to go outside since I'd already showered. Figured I'd fix it in the morning. I was at my desk. I'd finished an assignment and I was watching a video to get ready for another assignment. Planned to watch it then head to bed." He shivered. "I felt weird. Like the hair on the back of my neck stood up. I glanced up and he was right there. At the window. He had his dick out, holding it, and he smiled at me. Like a lewd smile. I screamed and ran to you."

My heart did crazy things as I thought about Keegan being scared, being in danger, and also that he ran to me for comfort and protection. I pulled him close. "Okay, we're going to call the police. I haven't checked the cameras in ages; the warning signs and visible cameras always seemed enough to keep intruders away so I've not really kept up with arming the house at night. But the alarm company can probably download camera footage from the cloud. And we'll start turning the alarm on at night, during the day, when we're gone, all of it."

Keegan sniffed and nodded.

Three hours later, both of us were exhausted from the whole ordeal. Waiting on the police to arrive. Talking to them and answering all of their questions. I'd hesitated when they asked if anyone else aside from the landscaping crew would have known Keegan was living here. Keegan had shaken his head; he clearly didn't want to get into his webcam situation. And really, it *did* make the most sense that one of the landscapers had come back. In order for it to be some random stalker from the internet, the person would have had to do *a lot* of hacking and digging. One of the Lawson's Landscaping crew members, or hell, even someone from the little garden shop who saw Keegan with me, was a more likely suspect. While the officer had been checking Keegan's room, I'd whispered, "If nothing comes up or it happens again, we're telling them about the video stuff."

Keegan had nodded and sagged against me.

I'd spent over an hour on the phone with the alarm company as they found, reviewed, and downloaded footage from my security cameras. The police would be investigating who and what were on that video.

The alarm company sent a service person out—I was

impressed they sent someone so late—to walk both Keegan and me through arming and unarming the alarm system.

When everyone was gone and we'd done all that we could, Keegan began to cry.

"Hey, it's okay," I whispered as I took him in my arms. "Tell me what's wrong."

His shoulders shook softly. "I can't sleep in there. Not right now. Not until I know he's not out there, won't be coming back."

"Of course not. We've got plenty of rooms. I'll help you move your stuff permanently if you want. But for tonight, take your pick. Upstairs or down?" I ran my hand up and down his back. I wanted to drag him to my bed, but I wasn't sure the gesture would come across as protective—possibly more like creepy.

Keegan turned sleepy, scared eyes up to mine. "Can I sleep with you?"

Okay, then. Not creepy I guess. With my stomach doing acrobatics of epic proportions, I nodded and kissed the top of his head. "But just to *sleep* tonight. Too much has gone on in the last however many hours to think of anything but sleeping."

Keegan nodded.

While he took a shower in my room, I armed the alarm, pulled all the blinds in his room, and gathered the belongings I thought he might need for an overnight in my bedroom.

Don't act like you're not seriously considering moving him in there on a more permanent basis.

Now wasn't the time for that. Keegan was scared. Hell, *I* was scared. I wanted him in my arms, in my bed—yes, for more than *just* protecting, but for the time being, that was all —tonight and for however long he wanted to stay.

I found Keegan, fresh from the shower, curled up on my bed. I placed a throw blanket over him and took my own quick shower before returning to the bed. "Hey, Kee, can you wake up so I can pull the blankets over us?" I nudged him gently and he jerked awake. "Sorry, just me. Let's get under the blankets."

Keegan murmured something and crawled to the head of the bed while I pulled the covers down and climbed in next to him.

"You good?" I asked, brushing the hair away from his forehead.

He nodded. "Yeah," Keegan whispered. "Can you hold me?"

As my heart melted, I opened my arms and let him burrow against me. Sex or no sex, I never wanted to lose the feeling of Keegan in my arms.

"Sexy time in the morning, m'kay?" Keegan mumbled against my chest.

"If that's the next step in *Keegan Take the Wheel*, I'm ready." I kissed the top of his head. "Maybe *ready* is the wrong word. Excited? Anxious? Scared to death?"

The only answer I got was a soft snore from Keegan.

I FELT Keegan get out of bed the next morning. It was early, but the sun was beginning to peek through the windows. When he returned, I took my turn in the bathroom—I could smell toothpaste and soap, so I did a little clean-up of my own before heading back to bed.

I crawled back under the covers and took Keegan in my arms. He sighed and rolled to face me.

"Sleepy morning kisses?" he asked as he nuzzled his nose against my neck.

I tipped his chin up and kissed him softly as my hand trailed down his back, over his hip, and cupped his boxer briefs-clad ass. No matter what Keegan wore, he was sexy. My hands would never get enough of touching him; my mouth would never tire of kissing him.

We kissed, soft and slow, for several moments and my dick was very interested in sleepy morning kisses and whatever might follow. "Good morning," I whispered as we broke the kiss.

"Morning," Keegan mumbled. "You want to do anything? Move slow? Super slow? Fast? Blow past the speed limit?"

"I thought you were making the decisions here." I squeezed his ass and kissed along his jaw.

"I'll decide what we do, but I want the speed to be okay with you."

"Kee," I started, but paused when he blushed. "Sorry, not okay?"

He shook his head. "I love it. No one has ever been close enough to me to call me that. I like that it's the name only you call me."

I smiled. "Okay then. *Kee*, we've been going slowly—like speed of frozen molasses slowly—for long enough." When he raised his brows in question, I plowed on. "I think I'm ready to wax my balls," I stated and then laughed at the look on Keegan's face. "Metaphorically speaking, of course."

He threw his head back and cackled. "I'm the man for the job, I promise. Metaphorically *and* literally if you ever decide to go that route." He kissed me. "You're on the table. I've got the wax warmed and ready to slather on your balls. Last chance…" his words trailed off as his hand ran down my chest to my hip.

With a ragged voice I barely recognized, I whispered, "Fuck, please don't let me screw this up. My heart couldn't take it." I captured his soft, warm mouth. When he gasped, I dipped my tongue in to taste him—mint and Keegan were a perfect flavor.

We made out for several minutes. Hands roaming, arms and legs tangling, lips and tongues teasing, nipping, and tasting. Keegan rolled to his back and pulled me on top of him. I'm not even kidding, settling between his legs was like finishing the last piece of a puzzle. Like the last number of a combination lock rolling into place. All my life, I'd been trying to fit my square peg self into incompatible round holes.

I snorted.

Keegan's bright eyes flashed and he smiled. "What are you snorting about?"

I nestled my hips between Keegan's and groaned as our hard cocks rubbed together. "This is going to sound dumb," I started.

"Nope. Nothing we do or say is dumb. We're learning each other. Learning brings questions." Keegan leaned up to kiss my chin.

"I was thinking that rolling over and settling between your legs was like the last piece of a puzzle. Like all this time I'd been a square peg trying to fit in round holes." I chuckled. "Then I thought that the metaphor contained *a lot* of sexual innuendo, you know with *pegs* and *holes*, and it made me laugh."

Keegan giggled and rolled his hips. "Not sure my ass can take a *square* peg," he teased, "but I'm all for my hole and your peg getting together."

I laughed again and kissed him. "Lead on. I am your willing scholar."

Keegan continued to laugh and clutched at my ass as he rocked his hips into me. "The professor is now the student."

"Damn good thing you're not one of *my* students. *That* would be a major problem."

"Well, we're done worrying about problems, right? We're here to learn and enjoy." Keegan smacked my ass.

I gasped.

"Interesting. My professor might like a little spanking." Keegan winked. "For real though, we are going to mess around this morning. We're both definitely getting off. But I want to do some real-talk about prep before we move to anything more."

I nodded. "Which first?"

"Well, Professor, I'd like to introduce you to *frottage*, better known as frotting in sexual terms," Keegan slid his hands under my boxers. "We're going to strip to bare skin, make out, and rub our cocks together until we come."

I swallowed thickly and nodded.

Keegan grinned. "Get naked."

I rolled from the bed, shucked my boxers, and licked my lips as I watched Keegan strip. My breath caught in my chest when he laid back and looked up at me with unsure, anxious, lust-filled eyes. "You're so damn gorgeous," I whispered and crawled onto the bed to lay beside him. I placed a hand on his shoulder, trailed my fingers down to his chest, and smiled as he gasped at the touch of my thumb on his nipple. "Can I just look at you? Touch you? I want to get to the cocks and coming and all that, but it's like I can't get enough of looking at you."

Keegan nodded. "Look and touch all you want." He took a quick breath and bit his lip as I continued to play with his nipples. "I've never been in bed with someone. In a school closet, behind a building, in a car, all very rushed and mostly clothed." He moaned as I bent to tease a nipple with my lips and tongue. "I wasn't prepared for how amazing being naked in bed with you was going to be. Hell, even just being in bed with you completely clothed is more than I'd ever imagined."

I licked and bit at both nipples before trailing kisses down to his belly button. Never before had I found a naked body so beautiful and enticing. I wanted to touch and kiss and lick every part of him. I traced his soft belly and smeared the drop of precum before moving to lick the slight V lines that led to his groin. My hand moved to his knee. I rubbed up his thigh, the light hairs on his leg tickling against my palm. My hand brushed against his balls and then his cock, and I paused to see if he was okay with the touch.

Keegan nodded. "Hands only right now, but God, yes, please touch me."

With my own cock harder than it had ever been in my entire life, I teased a thumb along his balls and up the length of his dick. I cupped his balls, played with them for a moment, and then moved to take his length in hand. He wasn't large, but I'd never seen a more perfect cock. "I want to taste you," I whispered.

"Not yet," Keegan chided with a breathless moan. "Later, you can. And after that, I'll have you straddle my chest just like this and feed that beautiful cock between my lips inch-by-inch." He bit his lip as I groaned. "But right now, I want you between my legs. I want to feel the warmth of your skin, the weight of your body against me." He spread his legs in invitation and I rolled on top of him.

"I'm not too heavy?" I braced myself on my elbows and took his head in my hands.

Keegan shook his head. "So perfect."

I leaned in to devour his mouth and groaned as he pressed his leaking cock against mine. "Oh shit, this won't last long," I warned.

"Same," Keegan agreed. "Rub yourself against me."

What started as a somewhat shaky, awkward rhythm soon turned into a perfect melody of thrusting hips and warm skin-on-skin as our cocks rubbed together. I took Keegan's mouth and savored the flavor of him on my tongue. When he ran warm, soft fingers down my back and gripped my ass, my balls drew up tight. "Fuck, Kee, I'm so close," I bit out.

"Me too." Keegan reached between us and wrapped a hand around our throbbing lengths. "Help me," he demanded.

I curled my much larger hand around his and we stroked ourselves. I brushed a thumb over his wet slit and then mixed his precum with my own. "Wanna see you come," I whispered.

Keegan whimpered and threw his head back as he spilled his release over our fingers. I followed right behind, my cum shooting onto his stomach as I groaned. "Fuck, Kee. *Fuck*. So good," I grunted as my cock continued to pulse.

Keegan lifted his head to place kisses along my neck, my jaw, and then he kissed my lips. "Wow, you're a quick learner. Guess we both are. That was a first for me as well."

"You were perfect," I murmured against his mouth. I rolled off him and ambled to the bathroom for a wet cloth. Once we were both cleaned up, I climbed back in bed and stretched out on my side to face him.

Keegan did the same. "I really like when you call me Kee," he whispered. "It's like our own little thing because no one else has ever called me that."

I kissed his nose. "I like it too. Your mom or sister never had a nickname for you?"

He pursed his lips. "No. The one thing I ever remember my mom saying about my name was something about how she shouldn't have wasted a good name on someone like me."

I clenched my jaw. "Fuck her."

Keegan shrugged. "It is what it is. She's gone. I'm moving on. I like my name."

"Does it have a meaning?"

He frowned. "I don't know. I guess I've never thought to research it."

"I've carved lots of name frames and plaques with the

name and meaning, so I'm always interested in what names mean. Like *Jacob* means *supplant* which means *to trip up or overthrow*. Not super interesting or fitting."

Keegan cocked his head. "I don't know, you've definitely tripped me up." He ran a hand down my side and cupped my hip. "I think your last name is more interesting."

"Oakley?" I wrinkled my nose.

"Yes, *Oakley*. Your last name has the name of a tree in it and you carve wood? So, definitely fitting." He grinned proudly.

"Huh, I'd never thought of that." I reached over him, pressing my chest to his and kissing his neck, as I grabbed my phone. "Let's see what *Keegan* means." I went to the site I mostly used when looking up name meanings and typed in *K-e-e-g-a-n*. Then I burst out laughing.

"What?" Keegan demanded.

I wiped tears from my eyes as I continued to laugh. "No name could have ever been more perfect." I handed him my phone.

Keegan read it, pursed his lips and rolled his eyes, but then he smiled. "*Small, fiery one*," he read aloud. "I don't see it. Doesn't fit me at all," he quipped as he tossed the phone back toward me.

I laughed harder. "Come here, my small, fiery one," I growled as I pulled him closer. "I believe we have some *prep* information to discuss before we can continue our learning expedition."

Keegan giggled and cuddled into my chest. "Okay, there's a lot of information to cover. We can't get to it all at once, so if you ever have questions just ask. I'm not an expert in all of it—and it's not exactly rocket science—but I do know quite a bit." He kissed my throat. "What do you know about prep?"

I pressed my lips together. "Well, there are a couple things I think of when I first hear the word. I didn't know until recently that PrEP with the capitals is a medication to prevent HIV. A student was going through a bit of crisis and one of the things he was the most worried about was losing the ability to pay for the medication. When I was clearly confused, he explained it to me." I ran my hand up and down Keegan's back enjoying the smooth warmth of his skin. "I also know that the word *prep* can mean stretching so there's less pain." I frowned. I *never* wanted to hurt him, not even just a little.

"Hey, stop frowning. The stretch and sting? The fullness? Those things shouldn't *hurt* when done right, but the little bit of pain isn't a bad thing. At least not for me. What else?"

"I don't know mechanics of it, but I think prep can also mean cleaning?" I raised a brow in question.

"Exactly right. You actually know a lot more than I was prepared for so that's great. PrEP is a huge advancement in the medical field to prevent the spread of HIV, but it doesn't protect against other STI's so don't forget that. Prep as in stretching is very important. It's always best to stretch and relax the muscle before shoving a cock—or anything else—in. And lube isn't a *necessity*, but it's always appreciated." Keegan took my hand and curled against me. "Oral sex as in blow jobs doesn't *require* prepping, but a good washing and general cleanliness is always good. Rimming—tongue in ass—may not *require* prepping for all people, but as either the giver or the receiver I've got to say that an extensive washing is a must. Now, anal sex requires more prepping than most other sex—and while that may seem like a *duh* statement, not all people seem to realize it. A douche or enema kit is a gay man's best friend—I'm not saying *all* gay men do it, but I know a large majority do. I've read some horror stories where men *wished* their partner had taken care of things beforehand. There are *several* brands on the market, but the main thing is that a person finds one that's easy to use and *works*. Now, I'm not going to go into minute details—you're smart enough to figure it out—but suffice it to say that the liquid goes in and you do that until nothing but the liquid is coming out."

"You've done that?" I asked.

"I have, yes. If I know I'm going to play with toys or something, I'll prep myself." Keegan glanced up at me. "If you and I are going to explore anal, I'll need to prepare."

"Do I need to?"

Keegan shrugged. "Do you want a cock in your ass?"

I thought about that for a moment. "I'm not against *your* cock in my ass. That's all I can answer for now."

"Fair enough." Keegan smiled. "I'm definitely more of a *bottom boy* but I wouldn't mind topping from time to time if you find you like it."

I frowned. "I don't have any enemas or prep products."

Keegan grinned and winked. "The grocery order comes today, right?"

I nodded.

"You'll have some then and I will *happily* be taking advantage."

"So, what do we do until then?"

"Well, I was thinking we shower. Blow jobs and rimming? We don't *have* to jump into everything all at once."

"Are you okay with this moving kinda fast?" I cupped his cheek.

Keegan nodded. "I am. I'd tell you if I thought it was too much. We're consenting adults. We're exploring and learning in a safe relationship. I think we're okay to set our own speed." He tweaked my nipple. "And as much as I love a good dildo in my ass, I can't wait to get your cock in me. But first, a good soaping before I suck you and tongue your ass."

"Fuck," I groaned. "You may kill me."

"But you'll die happy," Keegan quipped.

We took turns in the shower. As much as I wanted a

naked, wet Keegan in there with me, it was easier to clean the more intimate parts without an audience. I figured he felt the same. Maybe as the relationship progressed that would change.

As the relationship progressed? I thought about that for a moment. Nothing about the idea scared me in the least bit. Okay, the thought of Keegan someday wanting to leave scared the shit out of me. But the thought of being in a real relationship—with a *man*—didn't bother me. In fact, I smiled as I imagined walking into faculty functions with Keegan on my arm. Would he want that? Could we face our social anxieties together?

A bit later, Keegan padded from the bathroom, naked and flushed, and crawled onto the bed. "Eventually, we need to leave this room for food, but until then, I say we enjoy."

His lips met mine in a warm, wet kiss and we spent several minutes rolling around on the bed with our tongues in each other's mouths.

When we broke, I pressed my forehead against his. "Can I ask you something before your tongue is in my ass and I forget?"

Keegan giggled and nodded.

"Where does that fantasy of the cum dump scene come from?" I kept my hands on him in case he decided to pull away from the question. "It's not something I've ever thought of and, before meeting you, I would have likely said it wasn't something I was into. But hearing you describe it, I'm definitely intrigued. Even if it's not something that ever moves past the fantasy stage, I want to try to understand it."

Keegan's brows drew together and he bit his lip.

"It's something I've never tried to explain so I'm not sure I actually can. I think it started as a combination of wanting to be wanted, wanting to bring people pleasure, and wanting to get off. The idea of multiple anonymous cocks deep in my ass, their cum all over my back, all while a man I love watches—knowing he loves me enough and is confident enough in our relationship to give me that—it's kinda overwhelming. I don't want an open relationship. I don't want to cheat on my partner. Being fucked is a definite turn-on, but I think it comes down to more than that. I don't want *their* cum in me. I don't want them cleaning me up and taking care of me. I only want the man I love to come in me, to clean me up, to hold me and care for me." Keegan took a deep breath and blew it out slowly. "Wow. Saying that all out loud was a first. I'm sure a psychologist would have a field day with that one, but it's who I am and what I want." He shrugged. "It's not like I can't be happy without it. Fantasies are often best left to be acted out in the imagination."

I nodded as I processed his words. "So, you'd be interested in unprotected sex within a steady, loving, committed relationship?"

Keegan swallowed and nodded. "After that one disastrous experience, I got tested every month for a while. Now I get tested at least once a year—which seems like overkill since I doubt my toys are passing STI's—but I guess you can never be too careful. If my partner was comfortable with it and going without condoms was an option, I'd be interested in it."

I blinked as I imagined sinking my bare cock into Keegan's ass. "I was tested after each sexual relationship—even though we always used condoms—and I get tested yearly now. I'm clear if condomless is the way you want to go."

"Very much so." Keegan kissed my chin and then hovered over my lips. "But right now, I'm mostly interested in swallowing your cock and tonguing your ass."

I groaned. "Tell me what to do."

Keegan rolled to his back and moved to the head of the

bed. "Come straddle my chest. We *could* get out of bed and I'd drop to my knees to blow you, but that seems a little bland since we're already *in* bed and experimenting. So, bring that gorgeous cock up here," he patted his chest, "and feed it to me."

I almost swallowed my tongue as I clamored to follow directions. I climbed onto Keegan's chest and spread my legs. It could have felt awkward, but Keegan ran his hands up my thighs and gripped my hips as he licked his lips and stared greedily at my throbbing cock.

"Give it to me," Keegan demanded.

This type of sex was *nothing* like anything I'd ever experienced—yes, I was realizing my sexual history was very plain and boring in more ways than one—and I wasn't sure I'd last longer than one touch of Keegan's mouth on my dick. But I took my shaft in hand, stroked once, and tapped the plump head against his lips.

Keegan smiled and his tongue flicked out to taste me.

I grunted as his lips parted and allowed me to slip inside. The heat of his mouth would have brought me to my knees if I wasn't already there.

Keegan squeezed my hips and pulled me forward, my cock surging between his lips as I groaned. "Fuck, Kee. That's so good."

He pulled off and licked his lips. "You don't have to go gentle. I want it hard and deep." Keegan sucked me back into his mouth and guided my hips to thrust hard and fast.

With his warm, wet mouth engulfing me, his fingers digging into my hips, and his throat swallowing around me, I immediately knew I was going to blow very quickly. "Kee, I'm going to come. I don't want to go too fast."

"I want to taste you. Come for me. I'll get you hard again when I eat your ass," Keegan said before taking me deep again.

I braced my hands on the headboard and began to pump my hips harder and faster until my balls grew tight and I lost my load down Keegan's throat. "Fuuuuck," I roared as my cock pulsed. Looking down to watch Keegan take everything I gave him, I wiped a drop of my cum from the corner of his mouth as I pulled my spent dick from between his lips. I rolled from atop him and collapsed on my side. "Holy shit. That was fucking amazing."

Keegan wiped his lips and smiled. "Absolutely. I knew sucking you off would be amazing."

Although I felt like a rag doll, I lifted my head and glanced down at Keegan's still-hard cock. "Can I suck you?"

He blushed. "You don't have to. I can jerk off. Hell, I may even get off when I'm rimming you."

"But if I *want* to?"

"I'd never stop you from doing it," Keegan whispered and fisted his cock. "Just know that I'm not expecting you to do everything *I* do."

I shifted, knocked his hand away, and took his dick in my hand. "Tell me if I'm doing it wrong."

Keegan whimpered. "No way. Your mouth on me could never be wrong."

Flicking my tongue out to tease Keegan's leaking slit, I savored the taste of him for only a brief moment before taking his head in my mouth. I smiled around his cock when he moaned and thrust his hips up from the bed. His cock was the perfect size—a whole mouthful, but not so big as to gag me—and I appreciated that. Knowing how good Keegan's mouth had felt on me, and how good my own fist felt when I jacked off, I applied both to my very clumsy, awkward first blow job.

By the way Keegan was whimpering and moaning under me, I could only assume he enjoyed what I was doing. I placed my arm between his legs and elbowed him to open wider as I cupped and played with his balls. Sucking dick had never been something I longed to do, but I quickly realized that I'd be happy to have Keegan's cock in my mouth any time he wanted it there.

Keegan gasped and touched my shoulder. "I'm going to come. You need to pull off if you don't want it in your mouth," he warned.

I thought about it for a split second and increased my ministrations in anticipation of swallowing Keegan's cum. When he moaned, tensed, and thrust hard up into my mouth, I reveled in the warm, saltiness that burst onto my tongue as Keegan groaned my name.

I decided then and there that I would forever want to hear my name on his lips during orgasm—and when he was teasing me, laughing with me, talking about the most random shit. Hell, I wanted Keegan saying my name *always*. Knowing that *I* had brought him that pleasure was a very heady feeling.

I took Keegan in my arms and we cuddled together. "Was that okay?"

Keegan giggled. "I haven't had a whole lot of blow jobs, but I can assure you that it was one of the best orgasms of my life. Maybe because you're an excellent cock sucker, maybe just because it was with you, but it was fabulous and I will *never* turn down your mouth on me."

"Are you still wanting to do more before we leave bed for the day?" I ran my hand down his back and cupped his ass. "I'm not sure I can get it up again."

"Oh, a challenge. I accept." Keegan pushed at my chest. "But I want pizza and wine for lunch if I complete the challenge. Get on your hands and knees."

I laughed. "You can have pizza and wine for lunch even if you don't complete the challenge." I moved to my hands and knees and glanced over my shoulder to see what he was doing.

"Down on your elbows. Bow your back, spread your legs, and put your ass in the air," Keegan demanded. "If it's too much or you don't like it, let me know."

When Keegan's mouth pressed kisses against my ass cheeks, I shivered. When his tongue licked from my taint to the top of my crack, I cried out. For the next several moments—while I moaned and whimpered at his touch—Keegan's tongue teased, licked, thrust, and tasted as he stroked my limp-but-quickly-revitalized cock.

"Oh fuck," I bit out when I realized I was going to come again. "Shit, Kee. I'm gonna come."

Keegan blew a hot breath against my hole, pressed a thumb against my taint, and dipped his tongue into my ass until I shuddered and shot my release into his fist.

With no bones left in my body, I dropped to my stomach, barely even phased by the wet spot I settled into, and panted. "Not sure I have the energy to return that favor *right* now, but I definitely want to at some time."

Keegan's stomach growled. "Even if you wanted to, I'd need to be fed before anything else. I feel like I may pass out if I don't get food soon."

We made our way to the shower and washed off quickly before dressing and making a beeline to the kitchen. I poured wine and we set to work making pizzas for lunch. When the pies were in the oven, I settled in the corner of the countertops, and pulled Keegan to stand between my legs. "Thank you." I kissed him gently and cupped his ass.

He cocked his head. "For what?"

"For taking control, for helping me take a leap I wasn't sure I could take on my own, for teaching me. This has been amazing and I've loved every second of it." I kissed him again and hugged him close. "But I don't want you to think it's just the sex. I love spending time with you whether sex is involved or not. I'm so grateful you're here. And it's not just because I was lonely—anyone else using my guest room would have been just a guest. You've become a friend—and even more—and I'm so glad you're here."

Keegan's eyes were bright and shiny. "I'm grateful to you and glad I'm here as well." He kissed my chin. "The sex is a definite benefit," he teased.

We settled in to eat our pizzas and finish off our wine. The rest of the day was spent fixing the fairy garden, tending the vegetable garden, and talking to the police. The guy outside Keegan's window was one of the Lawson's Landscape employees. Keith had been arrested and charged. The police didn't expect that he'd cause any more problems.

"Do I have to move back to my room?" Keegan asked.

"Not unless you want to," I answered. My heart clenched as I worried that he'd want to go back to his own bed.

"I want to stay," Keegan said and took my hand.

My heart longed to know if his answer meant *stay* in my bed or *stay* with me after his time was up.

TEN

KEEGAN

"CAN WE MOVE MY GARDEN?" I asked a few days later. "I know we *just* made it and fixed it again, but if my window is now in *your* bedroom, I can't see my fairies." It was way too soon to say *our* bedroom, right? Honestly though, moving into Jake's room had seemed like the most natural thing in the world. I don't know if it was just his personality to make people feel so welcome—I didn't really think he would have ended up sleeping with just *anyone* who used his guest room...and even the thought gave me all kinds of jealous butterflies in my belly—but somehow, Jake and I had so easily fit into each other's lives. I was pretty sure Jake would have been happy to hear me say *our* bedroom and that I was having a shit-ton of thoughts about what our life together would look like after I graduated.

For real though? Aside from the fact that I'd be working instead of taking classes, I didn't think things would change that much. Maybe we'd work on increasing our trips to town, widening our social outings, or even get a puppy. Maybe we'd keep things exactly the same way they were at that exact moment. Either way, as long as I was with Jake, I really didn't care.

But maybe playing it cool for a while was for the best. There *was* such a thing about coming across as desperate and *too* clingy. I didn't want to be that man.

Jake pulled me into a hug. "Of course, we can. But I do have a favor to ask you. You can totally say no, but I wanted to run it past you before I made my decision."

I raised my brow. "Can we talk while we move the garden?"

Jake nodded and we headed outside. "Whoa, gonna be a hot one today if it's already *this* warm. Seems like spring has already given way to summer if these temps are anything to go by."

"That's why I wanted to get out here and get it done as early as possible." I gathered the twinkling lights, the ladder, and all the toadstools.

"You mean the anticipation of morning blow jobs wasn't what woke you up so early this morning?" Jake winked as he picked up as many tiny items as he could carry.

"Oh, the blow jobs were definitely worth waking up for. But once I was awake, I figured we could beat the heat." Once we had all the garden items carried to the little patch outside Jake's window, I stood with my hands on my hips and attempted to imagine how I wanted the garden to look. "Can you get—" I glanced up to ask Jake for some tools, but he was gone.

"Figured you'd need these," he said as he came around the corner a few seconds later with spades, gloves, a trowel, and a piece of foam for my knees.

My heart soared and I smiled through stinging eyes. "Thank you." Seriously, how did this man know me so well? And who knew how much of a turn-on it would be to be taken care of? And why the fuck was I teary-eyed over a hot, caring guy bringing me gardening tools?

I set to work and Jake sat on the ground next to me, handing me things as I needed them. "So, what's this favor?"

"Well, I got an email from the head of the university. There's a faculty awards dinner coming up. I don't *have* to go, but it's kinda frowned upon if I skip it. One year, I lucked out and had the flu. Another year, I was blessed with a kidney stone. The other years, I've gone and hated every moment of it."

My chest constricted. Did he want me to go? Was he going to ask if it was okay if he took a woman as a date? Could I even handle a faculty awards dinner?

"Kee? You need to breathe." Jake put a hand on my shoulder. "So, I can pretty much figure your answer here, but I want to make sure we're being open and honest. I don't *want* to go to the dinner, but I feel like I kinda *have* to. If I go, I'd really like you to be my date."

I took a deep breath. "Oh, shit."

"What? Too much? Too soon?" Jake winced. "I'm sorry. Maybe I shouldn't have asked you, but the moment I thought about going I realized that I wasn't so against it if you were with me."

God, this man.

"Why do you want me with you? Would I be a big fuck you to your colleagues? A way to avoid an annoying woman who wants more than you're interested in?" I realized I sounded like a jaded bitch, but I wanted to be more than that to Jake.

Jake shook his head and reached his hand out. "Come here, little fiery one."

My cheeks—already warm from the heat—burned and I pouted as I let Jake pull me into his lap.

"I want you with me because I like spending time with

you. I think you're gorgeous and I want to show you off. I hate social events and knowing you'd be by my side was a positive." He kissed my neck, my cheek, and then my lips. "These things are terrible to attend. Stuffy, boring, and long. I probably won't even win any awards."

"Well, when you put it that way, how could I *not* want to go?" I deadpanned.

Jake chuckled. "Yeah, I know, sounds like a terrific date night. I could go by myself, but I'd rather you be with me."

"Do you just want me there as a buffer against how much you hate it? Like, a female date would do just as well?" I bit my lip.

Jake frowned. "Why would I want a female date?" He took my chin and forced me to look at him. "Pretty sure we've determined that I one-hundred-percent do *not* want a female companion."

I shrugged. "So, ask a guy?"

He shook his head. "Why would I ask some random guy to go as my date when I have *you* right here? I want to take you because I know I'll have someone to talk to, someone who has my back, someone who will recognize if I need to get the fuck out of there. You are the only person I'd ask to be my date to something like this." He leaned in and kissed me. "If you don't want to go—if it's too much or too soon—I'll make a quick appearance and then we'll spend the rest of the night here in our own little bubble."

I frowned. "Is our bubble starting to confine you?"

"Never. I love our coziness, our routines, and our privacy." Jake nuzzled my neck. "But if there was *ever* anyone I could *maybe* see myself branching out with—maybe exploring a few social situations a bit more—it would be you."

"So, when is this dinner?" I pursed my lips.

"This weekend. Friday night." Jake raised his brows. "You want to think about it?"

"Can I order some new clothes?"

Jake smiled and nodded. "Of course."

I batted my lashes. "Can I wear a butt plug during the dinner and we can come home and have a lot more fun than some stuffy faculty dinner?"

Jake groaned. "Gonna fucking kill me, Kee. But, yes. You can wear whatever you want."

"What if I wanted to do my makeup?" I knew I was being kinda petty. I probably wouldn't have wanted to wear makeup to a faculty event, but I wanted to hear what Jake said.

"You can wear anything you want. I want you to know you're able to be yourself and you're safe. If we get there and either of us feels uncomfortable or unsafe, we'll leave." He pulled me close and captured my lips.

"Will there at least be good food?" I asked breathlessly when we broke from the kiss.

"It's usually pretty good. If not, we'll hit a burger joint on the way home."

"On the way home to bed where I'll suck your cock and you'll slide the plug out of my ass before slamming your cock in deep?"

Jake's breath caught. "You're trouble, you know that?"

"I think we need a new challenge. No anal until we survive the dinner. Gives us something to look forward to." I raised my brows as I waited for his answer.

He cleared his throat. "But we can do other stuff until then?"

I nodded.

Jake's eyes burned. "So, if someone had ordered a hand-carved wooden butt plug and dildo, he'd be able to maybe use the dildo on your ass but no anal sex until after the dinner?"

I swallowed thickly. "Did you order a hand-carved butt plug and dildo?"

Jake nodded and I kissed him, plunging my tongue in as he moaned.

"Tonight, we play with the dildo. Friday, I'll wear the plug. Then Friday night, you'll fuck me."

His nostrils flared. "Well then, sounds like we've got plans tonight. Better get your garden done and finish your school work."

"You've got class soon, right?"

Jake nodded and adjusted himself as I slid from his lap.

"Okay, you go get set up for class. I'll finish here and shower before I order clothes and get started on homework." I reached down to pull him to his feet. "Lunch?"

"Do you have webcam stuff to do tonight?" Jake asked.

I dipped my head. "I haven't been doing as much of that as before."

Jake frowned. "Why? Did I make you feel like you couldn't do it?"

"No, not at all." I wrapped my arms around his neck. "It's just kinda hard to get into dancing and jerking off for strangers when I have the sexiest, most amazing, *very* willing man in my bed."

"*Very, very* willing," Jake whispered gruffly.

"See? How can I turn that down?"

"Well, I'll never complain. But please know that I'd never ask you to stop doing something if you enjoy it."

"Fucking my boyfriend is what I enjoy," I quipped and then froze. "I mean...um, not that I think...oh shit...sorry?"

Jake beamed. "Don't ever apologize. I've wanted to call you my boyfriend for a long time, but I was worried it was too much, too soon." He kissed me. "Worried it made me an old creep trying to hook up with a younger man. But the more we're together, the less I see our age difference. I just see that we click like nothing I've ever experienced before."

"So, you'd be okay with it?" I bit my lip, my ears still on fire.

"I would be. And you?"

I nodded.

He took my hand. "Keegan Greer, would you do me the pleasure of being my boyfriend?" he whispered against my ear.

I wrapped my arms around him and nodded through tears. "I'd love to." *And I love you*, I thought to myself. We'd just agreed to be boyfriends, go on a public date, and use hand-carved wooden sex toys. I should probably keep myself in check and not overwhelm him too much. But gawd, I couldn't help it; I was totally in love with Jake.

After Jake went to set up for his class, I finished the fairy garden. I had to admit, it looked even better than the first one and I looked forward to cozying up in the window reading nook to read and enjoy my little garden's beauty.

I took a quick shower then sat down to order new clothes. I ordered sleek black satin dress pants, a fitted white button-up, a deep purple—almost black—blazer, and a new pair of black silk panties. I'd pair the ensemble with my shiny black dress shoes. I hadn't asked Jake about the expected dress, but I knew he'd tell me to wear what I was comfortable in. I knew I'd look spectacular and the faculty could fuck themselves if they couldn't handle what I was wearing. It's not like any of them would know I had on silk panties and a wooden butt plug stretching my ass so Jake could pound me when we got home. Some things were better left private.

I giggled and settled in to work on my homework.

When I was done, I'd take a nap and maybe watch a movie. After dinner, *my boyfriend* and I had a date with a dildo.

THAT NIGHT, after dinner, Jake took a shower and then told me the bathroom was mine for however long I needed. I loved that he respected the fact I'd need some time and privacy. I also kinda loved that we were sharing a bathroom despite the fact that there were multiple bathrooms to choose from.

When I walked out of the steamy bathroom, wrapped in a towel, I found Jake asleep on the bed with a gift bag beside him. I kept the towel on for the time being and climbed onto the bed to snuggle against Jake's chest.

"Oh hey," Jake mumbled. "Sorry, fell asleep. You want your gift?"

"What's it for?"

"Just because, I guess. Just something I thought you might like." He handed me the bag.

I pulled out the most gorgeous, hand-carved wooden organizer I'd ever seen. "Oh my God, Jake. It's beautiful."

"You can use it for whatever you want, but I thought maybe for makeup brushes and things like that." He smiled softly.

"I love it and it's absolutely perfect." I leaned in to kiss him. "Somehow, between the worry stone, the toadstools, and this, you were able to capture me perfectly. All of the pieces were so exactly right. Thank you."

"Can I tell you something and hopefully you won't freak out?"

I cocked a brow. "Um, I guess I can say I'll *try* not to freak out, but it really depends on what you're going to say."

Jake cleared his throat. "This isn't something that's fleeting or a fling for me. I've fallen completely head-over-heels for you and I don't want to think about when it may have to end. I want you here with me, permanently." He cupped my chin and brushed a kiss against my mouth. "And before the intimacy and emotions of sex get involved—well, involved any more than they already are—I need you to know that I love you. I love spending time with you. I want to take care of you. I don't want to go back to a life without you."

Tears spilled down my cheeks. "Say it again."

Jake smiled and kissed me, deep and hard. "I love you," he whispered against my lips. "I don't expect you to feel the same, but I needed you to know."

"Don't be ridiculous. I've had to stop myself from saying *I love you* at least three times in the past twenty-four hours." I moved the organizer and bag to the floor, then hiked the towel up my thighs so I could straddle Jake's hips. "When I came here, I thought I'd hide in my room, do my webcam gig, get through school, then say goodbye and never look back. Little did I know that my heart would get involved and we'd have this unexplainable attraction and connection." I kissed along his neck, his jaw, and then nibbled at his ear. "I want to stay. I still plan to graduate, get a job, and work toward becoming a licensed therapist, but I want to be here. I want to do it all with you by my side."

Jake ran his hands up my back, over my shoulders, and down my chest until he reached the towel at my waist. He cocked a brow and waited for my answer.

With a nod of my head, I wriggled out of the towel as he loosened the material and then tossed it to the floor.

"I believe I have a new toy that would very much like to meet your ass," Jake whispered against my ear.

I giggled, rolled from his lap, and spread myself on the mattress. "Get the lube."

Jake fumbled in the drawer and produced a bottle of lube and the most gorgeous hand-carved wooden dildo I'd ever seen. Of course, I'd never *actually* seen a wooden sex toy, but it was beautiful nonetheless. My ass clenched as I imagined

Jake sliding it in, breaching my muscles, and fucking me with it.

Jake held the bottle of lube out to me and poured some on my fingers before he slicked the toy. "Finger yourself," he demanded.

I reached slippery fingers to tease my hole and pressed one then another inside. When I slid a third finger in, Jake shifted and pushed my hand away.

"Stop me if it hurts at all," Jake murmured as he pressed the slick head against my opening. He spent several agonizingly slow moments working the piece into me.

I groaned as the wood stretched my hole and filled me. "So full," I panted. "Move it, go deeper."

Jake began to slide the toy in and out, going a bit deeper on each return, and I yelped when he hit my prostate. "You good?" he asked with a worried look.

"So good. Keep going. I'm going to explode." I fisted my cock and stroked. It was almost embarrassing how quickly the situation was bringing me to the edge. But it felt so amazing I couldn't be embarrassed.

Jake continued to fuck the dildo in and out of my ass and I was extremely tempted to say forget the challenge of no anal sex, give me your cock. But I held out with a sharp bite to my lip. I whimpered when I spilled my release onto my stomach as my ass clenched around the toy.

Once Jake had slipped the wooden piece from my ass, I rolled him to his back, straddled his chest as I faced his feet, and bent at the waist to take his cock between my lips.

"Oh fuck, Kee," Jake growled.

I knew the view would be something he'd likely never experienced before and I definitely wouldn't mind his fingers in my ass and playing with my balls as I sucked him off. I stroked his shaft as I licked and teased, then I took him to the back of my throat and savored every grunt and moan Jake had for me as he thrust his hips up to fuck my mouth.

Surprising even myself, I came again a few minutes later as Jake shot his load down my throat. As good as the orgasm with the dildo had been, coming with his fingers in my ass and his hand stroking my cock had been even better. I licked his spent cock clean and moved to lay beside him.

Jake took me in his arms. "You are fucking amazing," he whispered. He held me, stroking my back, kissing my temple, and murmuring sweet nothings against my ear.

And I fell in love with my strong, protective, caring man just a little bit more.

"YOU SURE YOU'RE okay with this?" Jake asked as he took my hand.

We stood facing an old building on the campus of Jake's college. I knew he'd take me right back home if I said I wasn't okay.

But I also knew that we looked damned fine in our dressy clothes. I knew that the ass play we'd had a bit earlier—accompanied by blow jobs and earth-shattering orgasms—as Jake had helped me slip the butt plug inside, had us both glowing like no spa facial ever could. And I knew I was looking forward to everyone knowing I belonged to Jake and he belonged to me.

Not to mention how excited I was to turn on the naughty, flirty Keegan as we endured the stuffy dinner.

"I'm good. You?" I asked as I squeezed his hand.

"Feeling the best I've ever felt when faced with one of these. We'll mingle, eat, watch the awards, and leave. Unless we decide we need out earlier." He leaned over and kissed my cheek. "Your ass feel okay?"

I smirked. "My ass feels stretched and full like a constant reminder of what's to come—pun totally intended. Can you imagine what some of your colleagues would think if they knew your sexy twink of a boyfriend was walking around wearing silk panties and a wooden sex toy up his ass?"

Jake groaned and took my chin between his thumb and fingers. "You, my little fiery one, are trouble with a capital T. I really don't care what the hell *they* may think. All I care is that the gorgeous, sexy-as-hell man I'm madly in love with is by my side and will later be spread out before me like a damn buffet. I'm nervous as all get out, but I'm also about to come in my damn boxers thinking about sliding into your body." He placed a firm kiss on my lips and then chuckled. "And most of them would likely need medical attention if they knew any of that."

"I changed my mind. I think we should skip this shindig and get home as quickly as possible," I teased.

"Don't even want the free wine and food?"

"We have free wine and food at our house," I quipped with a grin.

Jake groaned and hugged me close. "I love that you say *our* house."

"Well, I *do* look damned hot in this outfit so it would be a waste to miss showing it off. Let's go mingle and impress." I hooked my arm in his. "But *later* is what mostly has my attention."

"I hear that," Jake agreed.

We walked into the building, arm-in-arm and took the ancient elevator to the top floor. The ballroom was old yet extravagant. It reminded me of old movies with lots of deep golds and reds, heavy fabrics, and decorative marble.

"Professor Oakley, so good to see you this evening. I was worried you wouldn't be able to join us," a husky voice spoke behind us.

Jake turned us so we could see the speaker. "Doctor Kincaid, nice to see you as well. Keegan, this is Doctor Kincaid, head of the department. Doctor, this is my boyfriend, Keegan Greer."

If Doctor Kincaid was shocked or appalled, she did a very good job of concealing it. "A pleasure. I'm thrilled you both could make it. Be sure to get yourselves something to drink and mingle a bit. Dinner is in thirty minutes and the awards are *not* to be missed." She smiled politely and left us.

"Well, that went better than expected. There's only a few colleagues who *might* not be super welcoming, and we'll avoid them if possible." Jake shrugged. "The rest should be completely fine or at least not care at all."

"No need to avoid them on my account. I'd kinda love to queen it up and get a little dramatic with the haters." I bumped my hip against his.

"Noted," Jake answered with a smile. "Want a drink?"

"Definitely. Vodka tonic with lots of lime would be great."

Jake raised a brow. "No wine?"

"Mixed drinks are fun. We've got plenty of wine at home. Plus, things like this usually don't have the sweetest of wine."

Jake ordered us both a vodka and Sprite with lime—extra lime for me—and handed me one of them. "Sprite may not be as *sophisticated*, but it's sweeter and makes the drink better if you ask me."

I took a sip. "Very tasty."

"Jacob," a voice purred from our left. "What a pleasant surprise."

Jake tensed and I wondered if this would be one of the not-so-welcoming colleagues. "Barb, nice to see you. Congrats on your nomination again this year."

"Ah, yes. Thank you. I, of course, wasn't surprised to see

you nominated as well. Always a shame that only one of us can win the big awards, right?" Barb smiled condescendingly.

Jake smiled. "Always felt the peer-nominated awards were a bit pretentious if I'm being honest. I enjoy the student-nominated ones more." He moved his hand from my back and I had a brief moment of panic that he was going to give in to the pressure and fear and pretend I wasn't there.

Instead, Jake took my hand and gave it a reassuring squeeze. "Barb, I'd like to introduce my boyfriend, Keegan Greer. Keegan, this is Barb Rotrame. She's an icon in the department—really even college-wide—no one *doesn't* know Barb's name." Jake was laying it on thick and I caught on quickly that he was speaking very sardonically.

Barb—who either didn't catch on or didn't care as long as the accolades were being given—seemed torn between preening and wrinkling her nose at me. "Jacob, *really*? This must be a joke?"

Jake tensed again and gritted his teeth. "Not in the least bit."

"A *man*? And aren't you robbing the cradle a bit? Surely this is a midlife crisis of some sort?" Barb glanced at our hands. "Perhaps a sports car or coloring your hair would have been less...*damning* to your career?"

"My career is just fine, Barb. But thank you for your concern."

"A sports car?" I asked sweetly. "Oh honey, Jake doesn't need a sports car. He drives me *just fine*." I winked and sipped my drink.

Jake threw his head back and laughed. "We really need to mingle a bit more before finding our seats for dinner."

We walked away from a gaping Barb.

Three more introductions went splendidly and I loved seeing how liked and respected Jake was despite him not being the most social person at the college. It was clear his colleagues respected his work even if they didn't get to socialize with him much. It actually gave me a lot of hope that I could one day be respected in my field even if I wasn't the life of the party.

The last introduction before dinner had Jake sputtering and my inner jealous bitch wanting to come out to play.

"Nice to see you, Chris. This is my boyfriend, Keegan Greer. Keegan, this is Chris Aimes. We came into the college together." Jake made the introductions between me and a *very* attractive man who was about Jake's age if I had to guess.

Chris faltered only for a moment and shook my hand. "Boyfriend? Damn. I'm happy for you. Always figured it was just a matter of time before you found yourself. My loss is his gain, I guess." Chris's cheeks pinked and he gave a little nod before retreating to the dining area.

Jake stood in shocked silence for a moment before he whispered. "Well, I'll be damned. Never would have guessed that."

"He's hot," I whispered. "And your age." My claws were competing with tears as a very real reality set in. "Someone you'd have a lot in common with."

Jake shook his head and smiled. "He's not the man I love. He's not *you*, my little fiery one, so pack your jealousy away and rest easy." Jake kissed my cheek. "There's *no one* I'd rather have in my bed, in my heart, and in my life. Just surprised me is all. I had no clue Chris was gay."

"Well, you *were* pretty oblivious when I met you. Just took a little sexy silk and lace to wake you up." I winked and kissed his chin. "Let's eat. I'm starving. This food better be delicious."

The food was actually pretty excellent and by the time I savored the last bite of dessert, I was more than ready for the awards ceremony so we could bust out and head home. My ass was fully stretched and *so* ready for Jake's long, thick cock to slide inside.

"You okay?" Jake whispered.

"I'm good. Food was great. I'm just ready to get home and get fucked."

Jake nearly choked on his water and his fiery eyes met mine with a promise of what was to come.

Me. I was to come. Several times if I had my way. My ass clenched and I imagined what it would feel like to be filled with Jake's cum. Only a couple more hours—one could hope the ceremony wouldn't take *that* long—and I'd be spread out in *our* bed and thoroughly fucked. Over and over again if things went according to plan.

AN HOUR AND A HALF LATER, I giggled as Jake shoved me into the elevator and pressed me against the wall. He'd won three awards—two voted on by students and one voted on by colleagues—and I was so damn proud of him. We'd held hands and played footsie during the entire ceremony and the sexual tension was at explosive levels.

He'd blushed at my praise, smiled and shook hands with colleagues, and quickly rushed me from the ballroom with all sorts of growly words as he punched the *down* button.

Jake gripped my ass and plunged his tongue into my mouth. "You are the most amazing, hot, beautiful, perfect man in the world," he growled as he pulled his lips from mine. "Thank you for attending that with me. I love you." He kissed me again before straightening my shirt and jacket and brushing a finger down my cheek just in time for the elevator doors to open.

Once we were home, we each took a bathroom for prepping and showering. I'd taken care of *things*, showered, and reinserted the plug. I found myself leaning on my hands against the sink and staring at myself in the mirror. How did I get here? What if I'd turned down the chance to live with Jake? Was the thing between us going to cause trouble between my dad and Jake?

A million questions and thoughts pounded around my head, but the one that hit me the hardest was how loved, protected, and cared for I felt. I didn't have a ton of life experiences—and a lot of the ones I *did* have weren't all that great—but the dream of being in a stable, loving relationship with someone who cared for me and protected me and accepted me for *me* had always seemed like just that, a dream. I wasn't crazy enough to think Jake and I wouldn't run into obstacles—that was a normal part of being a couple—but as I stared at myself in the mirror, I couldn't help but smile. I'd stumbled upon my soul mate. I didn't go searching for him— because I didn't believe he existed. I didn't throw myself at him—okay, so I *did*, but only once I realized there was a mutual attraction. I didn't have to reel him in—it meant a lot to me that Jake had come to me of his own free will.

Hell, I wasn't even born for almost half of Jake's life. But somehow, someway, fate had brought us together. My dad and Jake were the least likely people to be best friends, yet they were. I wasn't the type of person to go live with a stranger, yet I did. And now I was madly in love with my dad's best friend and I never wanted to think about what life would have been like if we hadn't met.

I wiped a tear from my eye and sauntered to the bedroom. "One of these days, I'm going to dance for you in my silk and lace." I wrapped my arms around Jake's waist and kissed his chest, the hollow of his neck, his jaw, and then his lips. "Maybe I'll tie you up—make it so you can't touch yourself— and I'll dance for you. Tease you, touch you, spank you, and you won't be able to escape. You'll have to watch me. You'll be so achingly hard, dripping cum, and you'll beg me to let you come. But I won't allow it until you've sucked me off—just your mouth and tongue, no hands. Then I'll tease your balls, slide my fingers in your hole, and maybe even press my cock deep inside until you shatter and come all over yourself."

Jake shuddered in my arms. "You are such a brat," he growled. "All of that sounds amazing."

"But?" I batted my lashes.

"But for now, we have other things to do." Jake pulled me so tightly against his chest that I felt as if I could climb inside. "I'm really nervous. I don't want to hurt you. You tell me what to do and how you want things."

I bit my lip and studied his face. "Well, my plans include more than a one-n-done. But I think I'd like to start on my hands and knees."

Jake groaned and nodded.

I smiled. "You like that idea?"

"God, yes."

"I'd also like to ride you and possibly try missionary if you're into it," I suggested.

"Why wouldn't I be into it?" Jake frowned.

"Face-to-face sex sometimes bothers some people, makes them think it's too much, too intimate."

Jake crushed my mouth with a bruising kiss then he pulled back and cupped my face. "I want it all with you. I want to feel you, see you, experience everything *with you*. I've never in my life had such intimate experiences with *anyone* and I want that with you. Always."

I nodded, breathlessly, and crawled onto the bed. "Thanks to this gorgeous plug, I don't need a lot of stretching, but you can play if you'd like. I just have to say that this first time will likely be like a bull ride—eight seconds and done." I was only kinda joking. "So, I have no problem with wham-bam-thank you-ma'am on our first foray into anal."

Jake pressed a hand against the small of my back to guide me to my stomach. When he lifted my hips and spread my ass to expose the plug, I nearly swallowed my tongue in anticipation. He grabbed the lube and tossed it to the side of the bed. "I'm going to slip this from your body and fuck you with my tongue until you're begging," Jake whispered as he trailed a finger along my ass.

"Do it. I'm begging now. Just touch me, fuck me, do something," I demanded on a ragged breath.

My body immediately missed the fullness of the plug, but soon Jake's fingers and tongue replaced the empty feeling. His long fingers teased and thrust until he got just the right angle to brush my prostate. My entire body electrified and I cried out.

"You good?" Jake asked softly.

"God yes, so good." I pressed my ass back against his hand. "Please Jake, give me your cock."

"Get up on your hands and knees," Jake commanded as he clicked open the lube.

I shivered as he spread the cool liquid into my ass. My cock was a simple touch away from blowing. I bent to my elbows and buried my face in the sheet as Jake pressed the wide head of his cock against my hole. The heat and fullness were almost too much and I bit my lip as I whimpered.

What could have turned into just a quick fuck, soon became so much more when Jake's large, warm hands caressed my back, gently held my hips, and slowly stroked my cock. When he pressed me to my stomach, held me in his arms as he thrust into my body hard and slow, and placed kisses against my temple as he whispered how much he loved me, I knew that what could have been just sex had turned into love making and I bit back a sob.

"You are so fucking perfect," Jake murmured, pumping into my ass. "So hot, so tight. My God, Kee, I love you so much."

"I love you," I panted. "I want you to come in me. Wanna feel you fill me."

Jake's thrusts increased and he reached to stroke my throbbing length. "Come for me, Kee. Wanna feel your ass clench around me." He jacked me until I was near tears. When I cried out and came in his fist, Jake gave three more hard, fast pumps of his hips and roared as he spilled inside me.

Minutes—maybe even hours—later when we finally came back to earth, Jake chuckled. "Holy fuck, I never thought sex with you could get even better, but I was so very, very wrong."

"That was fucking amazing. When I can breathe again, we're definitely going for round two." I moaned as Jake's spent cock slipped out. I rolled to grab a towel for clean-up and then attempted to wipe up the wet spot I'd left on the bed. Within minutes, I was cuddled in Jake's arms and we were sound asleep.

We woke several hours later and I pressed Jake to his back as I crawled on top of him. I slicked him with lube and shifted so his cock was pressing against my hole. "I barely need any lube since you left all that cum in me," I whispered and then smiled when Jake growled. "Gonna ride you and paint my cum all over your stomach," I promised. Gasping as his thick head breached my hole, I slowly lowered myself on his hard shaft and began to rock my hips as I rode him.

Jake reached for my hips and held me as he thrust his cock hard and fast. "Oh fuck, Kee, I'm not going to last long. So, fucking gorgeous. Jack yourself," he commanded.

With Jake's long, thick cock railing my ass, I fisted my

dick and began to stroke. In mere seconds, an orgasm rushed through me and I moaned as my cum spilled on Jake's chest.

Jake groaned and gave one final thrust as his cock pulsed and spurted deep within me. He took me in his arms, pulled me to his chest, and kissed me long and slow. "I love you so damn much," he whispered.

"Same," I murmured. "Shower?"

In a zombie-like fashion, we stumbled through a shower. With a towel over the sheet to cover the mess we'd made, Jake and I fell into a well-sated and very deep sleep.

ELEVEN

JAKE

WHEN WE WOKE LATER, the sun was shining through the windows at an angle that meant we'd slept very late into the morning. My body was deliciously sore, my arms were full of a warm and cuddly Keegan, and my cock was well-rested and ready for more.

Sex before Keegan had always been bland and boring. It wasn't that it didn't feel good, but it had never sent electricity coursing through my veins and fireworks exploding in my chest. Sex with Keegan—our time in bed had been an exquisite combination of love making and pure and simple fucking—was an earth-shattering experience on several different levels. The physical pleasure was second-to-none, but it was more than that. The physical and emotional intimacy—the *connection*—we'd shared was something I'd never had and definitely never wanted to lose.

Instead of dwelling on what I'd possibly been missing out on all those years, I chose to be grateful that I'd found it with Keegan. I truly believed that sex with another man—while maybe showing me that sex could be better than what I'd had —wouldn't have come close to what I had with Keegan.

"Are you regretting things?" Keegan whispered as he stretched awake in my arms.

I kissed his temple. "Never. Just thinking how much I love you and how grateful I am to have found you." I squeezed him to my chest. "Also thinking we haven't gotten to that face-to-face sex just yet and I'm totally on board if you're not too sore."

Keegan shifted and pulled me on top of him as he spread his legs. "I'm only a bit sore—I think the plug helped a lot—but I should be fine as long as you make it slow and gentle this time."

I pressed kisses all over his face and captured his mouth with mine. I made love to his mouth with my tongue before reaching for the lube and slicking my dick. I pressed my cock against Keegan's hole and watched pleasure fill his face as I popped through the ring of muscle. Glancing down to see where we were joined rocked my chest with a fiery tightness and I shifted forward to wrap my arms under Kee's shoulders as I kissed him long and slow.

With Keegan's legs spread and lifted, his cock trapped between us, and my balls pressed against his ass, I began to pull out and press into him in a slow, gentle rhythm. "Keegan, I love you. I will never *not* love you. I want to spend the rest of my life loving you, protecting you, and laughing with you." My words broke with emotion and I continued to thrust.

"Oh God, Jake," Keegan whimpered. "I love you. Never want to live life without you by my side," he whispered. "Come in me, let me feel you mark me. Make me yours."

His words and the hot clinging heat of his ass drove me over the brink and I came with a soft cry as my cock spilled. I devoured Keegan's mouth as he whimpered and came between us. The gentlest orgasm I'd ever had was the most meaningful one because it was with Keegan, face-to-face as I stared into his eyes and saw the very same love I felt for him reflected back to me.

"I need to sleep for ten days," Keegan murmured.

I pulled from his ass and wiped us both clean. "We can sleep until our bellies wake us up." Opening my arms, I smiled as a sleepy and well-sexed Keegan scrambled to cuddle against me. "I love you," I whispered.

Keegan answered with a snore.

WE WOKE to a blaring siren piercing the air.

"The alarm," I yelled over the noise as I rolled from bed and pulled on a pair of boxers and picked up my phone. I knew the alarm company would be calling.

Keegan yelped and followed suit as he yanked on the black silk panties he'd stripped out of the night before. "Oh my God, make it stop!"

I grabbed a hunk of wood from my dresser. At one point, it had been a clock. Now, it was my weapon.

Keegan picked up a loafer.

I wanted to laugh, but the ear-splitting wail of the siren had all of my attention. *Holy shit.* I'd never had the alarm go off. It was an intruder, right? Or maybe just a bird or insect set it off. I rubbed my eyes with the back of my hand and moved toward the door. Turning to see Keegan—and his shoe —following me, I held up a hand. "Stay here," I mouthed and pointed to the room.

Keegan shook his head vehemently.

I raised a brow in silent communication of *Please, just wait here until I know what's going on.*

Again, he shook his head. This time with a jut of his chin.

I sighed and rolled my eyes. With a nod, I slowly opened the door and snuck into the hallway with Keegan plastered to

my back. I looked left and right, saw nothing out of the
ordinary, and headed toward the alarm panel.

When we rounded the corner, I jerked to a stop when I
saw a man, his back to us, frantically punching numbers into
the keycode pad. The moment I saw the shock of crazy, wild
hair, I sagged in relief. "God damnit, Doc!" I hollered over the
siren as I stalked toward the box on the wall. Once I'd
punched in the code—Keegan's birthday—the house grew
blissfully silent.

With my ears still ringing, I quickly accepted the
incoming call from the alarm company as Doc's wild eyes
took in the scene before him. Once I'd assured the alarm
people that there was no intruder, I tossed my phone on the
hallway table and ran a hand over my face. "What the fuck,
Doc?"

His wide eyes scanned over me and he shrugged. "I've
always had a key. I didn't know you'd set up an alarm." Doc
glanced toward Keegan. "Keegan, step away from him.
Whatever is going on here, you don't have to do this."

Keegan snorted.

I saw red. "What the actual fuck does that mean, Doc?" I
crossed my arms over my chest. I knew exactly what he was
insinuating, but I needed to hear him say it.

Doc moved to face me, toe-to-toe—which was only
slightly awkward with me in my boxers—and poked at my
chest with a strong finger. "Damn you, Jake-y. Just damn you.
I trusted you with my boy. And you've got him," he paused
and glanced between Keegan and me like he was watching a
tennis match, "fuck, I don't even know what you've got him
doing. But I trusted you. I told Keegan he'd be safe with you.
And you've taken advantage of him in the worst of ways."

With only a split second of thought, I stepped back, balled
my fist, and punched Doc square in the mouth.

Keegan gasped and stepped forward to stand next to me.

For one scary moment, I thought he'd move to Doc's side and not be honest about what was going on. I sighed in relief when he wrapped an arm through mine and leaned his head against my shoulder. "Dad, that was completely uncalled for."

Doc ran a tongue over his split lip and grunted—this wasn't the first time either of us had thrown a punch—and frowned. "He punched me!"

"You accused him of doing inappropriate things to me." Keegan paused and pursed his lips as if considering all we'd been doing in bed. "Okay, more to the point, you accused him of taking advantage of me and that's not at all the truth."

"He's *my* age. What was I supposed to think?" Doc asked petulantly.

"Maybe you should think about your damned best friend —a person you've known basically since birth—and realize that I'd never in a billion years take advantage of anyone, let alone my best friend's son," I growled and rubbed my sore knuckles.

"Dad, I'm a grown man. Jake and I haven't been doing anything non-consensual." Keegan leaned in and kissed my cheek. "I'm going to get dressed. Then maybe some coffee and breakfast?"

I nodded. "Doc, since you're dressed and presentable, can you start in the kitchen? We'll dress and be right out."

I left a dazed and confused Doc standing in the hallway and followed Keegan to our room. He met me in the bedroom with a humorously wide-eyed expression and looking sweet and sexy-as-hell standing there in just his silk and lace panties.

"Oh my God! This was not how I planned to tell my dad about us," he exclaimed with a giggle.

"Really? I think it was the perfect scenario. Went very well," I deadpanned.

Keegan laughed. "Can we shower? I'd prefer not to eat breakfast with my dad as your cum drips from my ass."

I growled and gathered him in my arms. "You're a brat. Yes, we need to shower. But quickly. We need to explain things to Doc. I can tell he's already out there growing outlandish stories in his head."

We rushed through one of the fastest showers on record, brushed our teeth, toweled our hair, and yanked on sweatpants and t-shirts before quickly returning to the kitchen.

Doc had coffee brewing and water heating. "You still like hot chocolate better than coffee?" he asked his son.

Keegan smiled and nodded. "Yeah, thanks." He walked over to his dad and held out his arms for a hug.

Doc's face showed a wave of relief as he pulled Keegan into a tight embrace. "Sorry if I've overstepped or screwed something up. I'm just not sure I'm following what's going on."

"We'll work it out. Let's take the fruit and donuts outside. We can eat and talk on the patio," Keegan suggested.

We settled at the patio table. Keegan's chair drawn close to mine, Doc's across from us. We each took what was likely supposed to be fortifying sips of our drinks, but I was still nervous and shaky as hell.

I cleared my throat. "I'd like to start, if possible?" I glanced to Keegan and he nodded.

Doc just waited.

"So, you're probably shocked to find out I'm bisexual—or maybe gay. That's still something I'm figuring out," I began.

My best friend shook his head. "No. That part doesn't surprise me at all."

"What?" I croaked.

Doc shrugged. "I always wondered why you were never as excited about sex as I was. Granted, I was sleeping with women *and* men—and loving both equally—so I just thought maybe you were asexual or gay, but it really wasn't my place to say anything."

"You could have suggested it," I interrupted.

"Yeah, I'm sure that would have gone over well. *Hey, best friend who doesn't really like to socialize, I think sex would be better for you if you tried some dick.*" Doc chuckled. "I'm really kinda surprised it took you this long to figure it out. I knew all about all of those crushes you had on guys way back then."

I shook my head. "Well, I guess things turned out the way they were supposed to." I smiled as Keegan took my hand. "Doc, I need you to know that I had *no* plans on Keegan's living here turning into *anything* more than just giving him a place to stay. The attraction between us hit me like a damn freight train."

"And he fought it, valiantly," Keegan interjected. "Annoyingly so. He was all *I'm too old* and *You're my best friend's son.* Blah, blah, blah," Keegan teased. "I'll admit, I was slightly worried that I'd mess up your friendship." He squeezed my hand. "But your lifelong friendship isn't what you thought it was if it can't withstand your son falling in love with your best friend."

Doc's eyes went wide as my heart almost exploded.

"In love?" he sputtered. "So, this is, like, serious?"

"As serious as a heart attack," I answered. "I love Keegan. Not just because he was a warm and willing body for his relatively short amount of time here. I love your son because he's a gorgeous person, inside and out, and I love every second I get to spend with him. I fall a little harder for him every single day. And—like father, like son—I find myself just wanting to make him happy and completely unable to say no to him."

Doc cocked his head to the side. "This is so fucking wild. You and I could have totally hooked up, fallen in love, spent our lives being more than friends." His nose kinda wrinkled and we both laughed at how *wrong* that seemed. "Instead, you fall in love with my kid. So, are we going to end up something like in-laws? Do I need to start bugging you for grandchildren?" His eyes went wide. "Holy fuck, my grandchildren will end up being my best friend's children. So. Fucking. Wild."

Keegan squawked. "Hold up. Let's not get too far ahead of ourselves. How about a grand puppy? Maybe we can think about a dog. I'm not ready for kids just yet."

I laughed and kissed his cheek. "I'm with you on that one. But a dog sounds like a great idea."

Doc narrowed his eyes. "So, if I were to stand up right now and demand you pick me as your best friend or Keegan, which would you choose? Is my son worth losing our friendship over?"

I stood.

Doc stood.

"Doc, I love you. You've been my best friend, my brother, my rock all of these years. But there are two things I need to say. One, you'd never put your best friend or your son in that situation." I crossed my arms. "And two, if it ever actually came down to that, I'd be devasted to lose our friendship."

"You'd pick Keegan?" Doc asked, his voice gruff.

I heard Keegan take a breath.

"Yes, I'd pick Keegan. Maybe it's selfish, but I've spent my entire life feeling like I was missing out on *something*—never knowing just what that was—and I've found it with Keegan." I smiled down and kissed the top of Keegan's head as he stood to hook his arm in mine. "We're kinda the perfect match. We complement each other, balance each other out, and just fit together like no relationship I've ever disastrously even attempted to be in."

Keegan wrapped his arms around my waist. "I love him,

Dad. And it's not one of those teen dramas where the too-young child screeches *But I love him*! I know I look young, I know in the grand scheme of things I *am* young, but I've been through a lot. I know what toxic and dangerous relationships are like—I've experienced more than one and I've seen the traumatic fallout of them. I know myself and I continue to learn about myself. I know that Jake is a very special person. He's never once made me feel bad for being *me*. He accepts me for who I am. He loves me, cares for me, protects me, and just wants me to be happy."

"I do all of those same things," Doc interjected a bit pouty.

Keegan snorted. "You do. And I appreciate that. But Jake also dicks me down in ways I definitely don't want discuss with my father." He pursed his lips and tapped his chin. "Unless you want details?"

"No!" Doc and I both yelled.

"That's what I thought," Keegan quipped.

"Dear God, I will never be able to unhear that," Doc mumbled.

"Similar to how I will never be able to unsee your bare ass fucking that Mindy girl way back in high school. A guy shouldn't know that much about his best friend's balls." I pretended to shudder.

"Touché," Doc amended. "Can we agree that the bedroom stuff stays between just the two of you. I'm an open-minded, free-spirited guy, but I gotta draw the line at knowing sex stuff about my best friend and my son." He cleared his throat. "Buddy stuff is good. Parenting stuff is good. *Anything* is pretty much good. But just no sex talk."

"So, you can keep the key, but maybe let us know next time you're going to be in town and want to visit," I suggested. "The alarm is a rude awakening."

"Why *do* you have an alarm? And what's the damn password? It's not your birthday or mine." Doc frowned.

"I've had the alarm system for a while, just never set it. We had a bit of a peeping Tom incident that made us both feel more comfortable setting it. The guy was caught quickly, we just like knowing we're safe inside." I moved slightly so Keegan and I could both sit back down. Doc followed suit. "And the passcode is Keegan's birthday."

Doc's eyes went soft. "That's kinda fucking sweet."

Keegan kissed my cheek and I blushed. "I have my moments."

Doc ended up staying for the week before he was swept off to some faraway destination. I adored seeing Keegan and his dad forming memories and bonds. I hated that they'd missed out on being in each other's lives for so long, but I was truly grateful that I got to watch their relationship grow.

On his last day at my place, Doc and I sipped coffee on the patio while Keegan slept in.

"I never expected this," Doc began. He gestured toward the house where Keegan was thoroughly sex-sated and curled up in our bed. "I knew without a doubt that you'd care for Keegan and keep him safe. I never hesitated in knowing you'd accept him—hell, if you could put up with me all these years, I knew you could welcome him. But I never expected to see my son and my best friend fall in love."

I cleared my throat. "I'm sorry if it's hard for you, but I can't change it and I wouldn't even if I could. I love him so God damned much my chest aches with it. I promise I will spend the rest of my life loving him, protecting him, and making him happy."

Doc nodded. "I believe that. It was a shock, but watching the two of you together has been something damned special, I've gotta admit. I've never once seen either of you as happy, settled, *peaceful* as you are with each other. After the surprise wore off, I'm man enough to admit that seeing the two of you in love with each other is one of the best things I've ever witnessed in my entire life." He took a drink and blinked back tears. "I got him late. I know I'm not perfect father material. But I love that kid like my next breath." He stared straight at me. "And I love you the same. Knowing the two of you have each other makes me happier than I ever could have believed. Take care of him. Show him the love he missed out on for so long."

I swallowed back tears and nodded.

"Do you regret not knowing—or not admitting it—way back then?" Doc asked in reference to my sexuality.

I was quiet for a moment before I shook my head. "No. I kinda hate that I was as miserable and confused as I was. But without all of my past, would I have ever met Keegan? He and I work together so well because of who we are. We wouldn't have been the people we are today without our separate—sometimes shitty—histories. So, no. No regrets."

"I'm proud to call you my friend. Watching you with him, knowing you're in love and happy, it does this old heart good."

I smiled. "Don't mention old. Sore spot." I winked. "*Keegan* does this heart good," I murmured and rubbed my chest. "I'll never regret my past, but I'll forever be grateful for Keegan showing my oblivious ass the truth."

Keegan's arms wrapped around my neck, his skin still warm from sleep, and he kissed my cheek. "All you had to do was let love in."

I turned and kissed him long and slow until Doc cleared his throat. "Not just *any* love. Just yours."

Keegan giggled. "And just think, it only took some silk and an unlocked door."

Doc groaned. "Oh my God, do I even want to know?"

Keegan grinned like the little brat he was and raised a brow my way.

"No, that's a story you'll *never* want to hear," I assured my best friend and swatted Keegan's ass.

EPILOGUE

KEEGAN

One Year Later

"Why are you being so weird?" I eyed Jake suspiciously as I sat on the ground with Cocoa and Bruno.

Cocoa was our chocolate Lab rescue we'd had for about a year. As soon as my dad had left from his almost-disastrous impromptu visit, I hadn't been able to keep my mind off of the possibility of getting a puppy. Jake had patiently driven us from shelter to shelter for almost a month as I searched for the *just right* dog to speak to me.

I'd found her the very moment I'd laid eyes on Cocoa. She'd been badly injured in an *accident*, but the way the poor thing shook and shivered, I knew there was no way it had been anything but intentional. We'd filled out the paperwork on the spot and taken her immediately to a vet who came highly recommended.

He'd taken one look at the young pup and offered that if I ever decided I didn't want her, he'd take her in a heartbeat. Cocoa had that effect on people. *As if I'd ever not want her.* He'd examined her stitched-up lacerations, burns, and bruises, and announced that with time and love she'd heal just perfectly.

Time and love were things Jake and I had plenty of. We spent hours and hours cuddling with her as she healed from her physical wounds. Jake hired a trainer to help Cocoa and us learn safe and productive procedures as well as ways to help Cocoa heal emotionally and mentally from her traumatic past.

Cocoa would always have some patches and scars where her beautiful brown fur wouldn't grow, but she'd healed completely aside from that. She hated stairs—although we'd gotten her *mostly* over that fear—and she did *not* want to ride in the back of Jake's truck—something we hadn't made a single bit of progress on and had decided not to push. But Cocoa was the sweetest, most well-behaved, lovable dog I'd ever had the pleasure of knowing.

And she wasn't too keen on our newest addition.

Bruno.

He was a spunky, energetic, cute-as-fuck-but-didn't-listen-worth-a-shit beagle mix puppy we'd gotten from a lady at the garden store just over a month ago. Bruno was not yet well-behaved, but he *was* super sweet and lovable.

Cocoa just wasn't all that sure she was pleased with his constant presence or incessant energy. She loved to go out and chase rabbits or a toy, catch a ball, swim in the creek, go for a walk. But Bruno's energy level was that of the Energizer Bunny—he never stopped. We kept assuring Cocoa that he'd eventually catch on to the training and grow out of his boundless energy. She didn't seem to believe it if the eyes she gave us were any indication.

Bucko was *not* a fan of either canine addition. We mostly kept them out of the office because the bird wasn't shy about letting his dislike of the dogs be known. It was kinda cute though to see Bruno cock his head in curiosity as Bucko cursed him out.

"Huh?" Jake's head popped up, eyes wide. "What do you mean?"

"You seem weird. You're all jerky and buzzed. Like you're worried about something or high. What's going on?" I'd noticed it for a couple days; Jake's weirdness had been even more pronounced that day.

He took a deep breath and sighed. "So, you know your birthday is coming up, right?"

"Yeah?"

"Well, I made plans for us. And the plans are for tonight."

"Tonight?" I squeaked. "Who's going to watch the dogs? What about Bucko? Why is it tonight?"

"Doc is coming over to stay with the dogs and Bucko. He's going to stay until the weekend. It's tonight because I feel like it may be best to do it before you've officially graduated and have your trauma informed care certificate." Jake nervously ran a hand over his face.

"Um, okay," I drawled. "And why is that?" Nervous anticipation jolted through me. Jake and I had been on several dates over the past year, but he'd never dropped one on me so suddenly. "And where are we going? What should I wear? How long do I have to get ready?"

"Let's go inside," Jake suggested.

"Oh my God, are you taking me on a date to divorce me?" I squawked.

He laughed. "Dramatic much?" He pulled me to my feet and wrapped me in his arms. "One, we're not married yet so no divorcing."

I shivered as the word *yet* washed over me.

"Two, this took *a lot* of planning and it's kinda intricate, so I'd like to be inside and focused when I tell you about it."

I arched a brow. "Okaaaay." I walked through the door and called for the dogs.

Cocoa immediately went to her bed. Bruno bounced

around like he'd eaten ping-pong balls before glancing between me, his crate, and Cocoa.

"Bed, Bruno." I pointed to his bed. The puppy sniffed and took the long way of getting there, but he eventually snuggled up in the smaller bed next to Cocoa's.

I turned a wary eye to Jake. "I'm not sure whether to be super excited and pumped or very scared and worried." I looked toward the couch and then down the hall. "Is this a conversation that can't be had in front of the children?" I whispered.

"Sit down, you brat." Jake took my hand and led me to the couch.

I sat and stretched my legs over Jake's lap. It was our usual position unless I was curled against his side or straddling him. "Okay, we're going on a date. I need details."

Jake worried his bottom lip. "This seemed like such a good idea until now. I'm going to tell you everything, but I need you to tell me exactly how you're feeling about it and if *any* part of it doesn't seem right, we'll cancel it and just go to dinner."

I frowned. "Well, you definitely know how to set the stage with equal parts intrigue and anxiety."

He took my hand. "Remember when you told me about your fantasy? The one where you'd be in a loving, stable relationship with a man who wanted nothing more than to care for and protect you and make you happy?"

My heart was immediately in my throat and I could only nod my head.

"We've been together over a year now. You're *it* for me. I love you so damn much it hurts sometimes. I can't say that I completely understand your need to have other men fuck you —and there's a pretty large part of me that's needed to take the last year or so to overcome the jealousy and just focus on the kinky hotness of it. But I can completely understand the role I'd play in your fantasy. There's nothing I want more in life than to take care of you, make you happy, protect you, and love you." He paused and lifted his eyes to meet mine.

"Jake, I'm going to need you to use very simple language here. What are we doing tonight? Because part of me feels like you may be telling me you planned a cum dump scene for me, but another part thinks you'd never do that, so before I pop a boner and come all over myself in anticipation," I squeezed his hand, "I'm going to need to know *clearly and concisely* what our evening is going to consist of."

"Do you love me?" Jake asked.

I smiled. "Of course."

"And we trust each other, right?"

I nodded.

"We're committed and stable?"

My eyes watered. "Yes, more so than I ever dreamed would happen for me."

"You still get turned-on by the thought of strangers fucking you, coming on you, and then me cleaning you up before sliding inside and coming in you?" Jake's gruff whisper and detailed words had me hard in an instant.

I breathed deeply through my nostrils and nodded. "So much," I murmured.

"Well, I've got something set up to make that happen."

I nearly fell off the couch. "How? Who? Where?" I sputtered.

"Remember Chris Aimes from the staff dinner?"

I crossed my arms over my chest. "I'm not letting a guy who has a crush on *you* fuck *me*. That is *not* my fantasy."

Jake laughed. "Relax. Chris is very happy with a new boyfriend. He and I are just friends. He knows I'm head-over-heels for you." He winked. "However, I never knew Chris had such an *in* with kinky shit. When I started thinking about making this happen, I dropped a few probing questions and almost fell over when Chris started listing all the ways I could set up a cum dump for you."

I put a hand over my face. "Oh my God, *Chris* knows? Your work friend, Chris? How am I supposed to see him ever again?"

"Chill. Out. *He's* the one who knew all the insider information, so I doubt he's completely vanilla. Plus, I'm pretty sure he met his current boyfriend at something very similar." Jake cupped my face and leaned in to press a kiss against my lips. "*Anyway*, he helped me get the details ironed out. We're going to a very nice downtown hotel—we're spending the night there and won't be home until late tomorrow night—and we're going to make your fantasy come true."

I could barely breathe.

"Unless I took it *way* too far and you don't want to do it," Jake rushed on.

I shook my head. "No, no. It's perfect. I never thought I'd be in a relationship where a man would love me enough to make this happen for me. I'm kinda blown away." I stroked a thumb over his knuckles. "Are *you* sure you're okay with this?"

Jake nodded. "I'm equal parts sure I'll see fire when they fuck you and nearly blow my load at the same time. But knowing you want it, knowing you'll be loving it, knowing *I'm* the only one who will be fucking you bare, marking you as mine, and *loving* you? All of those things make me one hundred percent sure that I'm okay with it." He shrugged. "Nervous **as** hell, but excited."

"And you wanted it done before I receive my certificate?"

"I'm not saying it's a one-and-done thing never to be visited again, but I keep having this worry that someone would find out and you'd somehow lose your certificate or even your chance to be a licensed therapist down the road."

"That's probably really smart thinking," I admitted. "Maybe I'll find out that this is all best left to my fantasies anyway." I kissed him. "But I definitely want to try it at least this once."

"We'll leave around six. Your dad just thinks we're going for a night away for your birthday and graduation rolled into one. I clearly didn't tell him about the other."

I laughed. "Probably a good idea. Not sure Doc needs to know." I glanced at my phone. "So, I have a *ton* of getting ready to do. Prep, shower, hair, makeup, butt plug, clothes," I rattled off. "Ack! I've got to hustle."

Jake smoothed a hand over my arm. "Relax, you've got plenty of time. Let's eat lunch and take a nap. Then you can do all the primping and prepping your little heart desires." He paused. "Oh, do you think you want to be blindfolded during the scene or do you want to be able to see?"

I mulled it over for a bit. "I *always* thought I wanted to be blindfolded, but I think I've changed my mind."

"Why?"

"Well, the thought of glancing over my shoulder to see whoever is fucking me *is* a turn on," I rattled, "but the idea of watching *you* as you watch me is even more so. And when the fantasy first formed, I wasn't picturing *you* in it. But now that I know it's *you*, I want to be able to see your eyes, your body, your dick as you slide it between my lips."

Jake groaned. "Keep talking like that and I'll be done before we even get started."

We ate a light lunch and took a cuddly-warm nap before I shooed him from the bedroom so he could entertain my dad as I prepared for our evening.

Two and a half hours later—what? It takes effort to look this good—I did one last check of my lined eyes, feathered my hair into place, and brushed a tiny piece of lint from my black zippered jeans. I'd rolled the jeans and paired them with a kitten-heel lace-up black boot, a dark gray, shimmery, asymmetrical tank, and a fitted black leather jacket. With a bag for clothing and a bag for sex toys and supplies in hand, I sashayed my butt-plug-stretched ass to the kitchen where Dad and Jake were chatting.

Jake paused and smiled. "You look amazing," he whispered gruffly against my ear as he pulled me close. "Let me take those bags to the car."

"You do look great," Dad added when Jake had left the room. "Never thought I'd see the day when I'm jealous of my son and best friend for the time they get to spend together." He frowned. "This is real, right? You're not just doing it to prove something or get your grandpa's money or whatever?"

I sighed and rolled my eyes. "Yes, Dad, it's real. It's never been about the money. I'll be happy to get it and put it aside for savings, but Jake and me have never been a means to an end or something that needs to be proven. I love him and he loves me and that's all we need." This seemed to be a conversation we had every time he visited.

Dad nodded. "Okay, okay, I hear ya. I really am happy for you. You guys have fun," he said and my ears caught fire, "and don't worry about the pups at all. We'll be fine here while you're gone."

I gave my dad a hug and took Jake's hand as he came back to walk me to the car. We chatted easily on the drive and I was surprised at how at-ease we both seemed to be with our fantasy evening ahead of us.

Once we checked into the room and unpacked, Jake pulled me to the bed.

"Let's make sure we have a plan and we're on the same page," he suggested. "The guys should be here in about thirty minutes."

"Do they know each other?" I asked.

"I think two of them do, but more like acquaintances.

They all three assured me they had clear STI tests, but since you're using condoms it wasn't as much of an issue." Jake ran a thumb over my hand.

"So many people have so many fantasies," I mused. "I'm not sure why mine always revolved around condoms being ripped off so they could come on my back, but it makes it easier to be sure safe sex is practiced." I glanced at the bed. "So, this bed is pretty tall. I think bending over it would work perfectly. Oh! Are these guys getting paid or is the experience payment enough?"

"Chris said it differed from participant to participant, but these three all stated that the experience was all they were in it for. There were three or four others who were interested and wanted cash payment, but their schedules didn't work with ours." Jake picked at the comforter. "Where do you want me during this?"

I crawled into his lap. "By my side the whole time. Touching me, talking to me, feeding me your dick. One of the biggest turn-ons of this fantasy is you and me interacting personally and intimately while the random, impersonal, strangers fuck me. I want to watch you, suck your dick, and tell you what I'm feeling."

"Do you want to come while they are fucking you?"

I shrugged. "If I do, fine. If not, fine. Either way, I'll be more interested in coming with you later."

"You want to know names?"

I shook my head. "Nope."

We took the next ten minutes to freshen up before there was a knock at the door. I stripped and bent over the side of the bed while Jake went to let the men in. My cock plumped against the mattress as three very attractive men entered the room. I smiled and licked my lips, letting my inner minx come out to play as I thought of the three dicks I'd be taking within the next several moments.

"Just to review the plan. Condoms will be worn. You can kiss his back, but no mouth. You can slap his ass," Jake said, but he glanced to me for confirmation.

I nodded and bit my lip.

"You can touch him, hold his hips, talk dirty to him. But you don't come in him. Pull out and remove the condom. Come on his back. Once you have the condom off, there's no pushing back in." Jake stripped his shirt and pants off. "You can stay and watch the other guys or get dressed and leave. Once you've all finished, you'll need to leave. If at any point during the scene anyone feels uncomfortable, the safe word is Doc." He caught my eye and winked as I giggled softly. "Any questions?"

I shook my head and glanced at the three men. They all shook their heads and began to strip while Jake put three condoms and a bottle of lube on the bed. When he returned to the bed and stood behind me, I wriggled my ass for him.

"He should be all stretched and ready for you," Jake murmured as he played with the plug, sliding it in and out of my ass a few times. When he removed it completely, I whimpered and immediately longed for the full feeling again.

With Jake on the bed to my left, I took his cock in hand and licked his dripping slit before glancing over my shoulder as warm skin touched mine.

The man gave me a wink as he rolled the condom down his impressive length and dribbled lube in my ass. He was broad across the chest with a trim waist and large thighs. When his cock pressed against my opening, I moaned and took Jake deep to the back of my throat. Humming, I let Jake rock his hips as I sucked his cock, but I pulled off with a gasp as the stranger's cock breached me.

"Okay?" Jake asked as he trailed a finger down my cheek.

I nodded and panted. "Just longer than I realized." The man began a hard and fast rhythm, his hands gripping my hips, and his cock brushing my prostate with each thrust. "Oh fuck," I moaned as electric shocks zinged through my body.

The man was breathing hard as he pumped his hips. "Gonna come," he warned.

"Pull out," Jake commanded as he smacked his cock against my cheek.

The stranger pulled out, stripped the condom, and shot hot ropes of cum onto my ass and back with a roar.

As he moved away and the cool air met my skin, I shivered. My cock was rock-hard against the mattress and I wanted to roll to my back and beg Jake to suck me, but the next man stepped behind me. I threw a look over my shoulder and took in his dark skin, his breathtaking smile, and his thick cock as he rolled on the condom.

The wooden dildo had nothing on this man and I whimpered and panted as he worked his substantial girth into me.

"You good?" Jake asked as he glanced back and forth between my face and the man who was fucking me.

I nodded. "So big," I gritted out.

"Too much?"

I shook my head and Jake nodded toward the man.

The stranger began to thrust as he ran a hand down my back and smeared the cooling come into my skin. "You like this big fat dick tearin' you apart?" he asked gruffly and I could only whine and nod. He drilled my ass for several moments as Jake kissed my lips and whispered how much he loved me.

"You're taking their cocks so well, Kee," he whispered. "But they don't love you like me."

I cried out and shook my head.

"They don't care about you. They're not going to clean

you up and protect you and make love to you, are they?" Jake crooned.

A tear slipped from the corner of my eye.

The man behind me pulled out quickly and grunted as his hot cum splattered all over my lower back. He moved to the side and was replaced by the third man.

The first two guys stayed to watch and I had to reach down to squeeze my dick in hopes of staving off my orgasm. I'd decided I wanted to save it for Jake. I turned to look at the third man and sighed in relief when I saw a very regular cock protruding from a thatch of red pubes.

I turned my attention back to Jake, moaning into his kiss as the third stranger sank into my well-used hole.

He leaned down and kissed my neck and back before whispering, "You're such a dirty little slut taking all these dicks and making your man watch." When he smacked my ass, I cried out before Jake shoved his tongue back into my mouth.

Whether the final guy had little stamina or he was as turned on by the scene as I was, he pulled from my ass all-too-soon and groaned as his release spurted onto my back.

Within moments, the three men were dressed and out the door. Jake moved quickly to the bathroom and returned with a wet cloth. "You okay? Was it good?" he asked as he ran his finger through the three men's cum on my back.

"So good," I whispered. "But all I really want is you," I answered honestly.

Jake wiped my back clean, pulled down the bed covers, and rolled me to the middle of the mattress on my back. I spread my legs and sighed contentedly as he took his place between them and our dicks rubbed together.

"That was so fucking hot," Jake growled, "but my head and cock are screaming at me to fuck you, come in you, show you that you're mine." He rocked his throbbing shaft against mine.

"Do it," I begged. "I need you in me."

Jake shifted and pressed the engorged head of his dick against my wrecked hole. "I'm going to fuck you like those men can *never* have you. Even when I'm pounding your perfect hole and filling you with my cum, I'll be making love to you. You're mine, not theirs. I love you," he whispered as he filled me. "I take care of you and keep you safe, not them," he growled. Jake moved so that his chest was against mine and I wrapped my legs around his waist as he thrust into me over and over.

Jake's arms wrapped under my shoulders as he anchored himself to me and increased the pumping rhythm of his hips. "Look at me," he demanded.

My eyes flew open and I stared at him.

"You're mine. No one else will ever come inside you," he bit out.

I nodded as another tear escaped my eyes. "I love you, Jake. I'm yours. You're mine. Make me come, fill me." I was only moments away from exploding and each thrust of his hips brought me closer to release.

Jake slowed his pace and held my face in his hands. He devoured my lips and made love to my tongue as he fucked me hard and slow. As his tongue thrust into my mouth, my balls drew up tight and I came with a whimper. My hot, slick cum coated our skin as Jake pumped his hips once more before releasing his load deep in my ass. My ass clenched, milking every drop from him, as I rode out the orgasm.

Jake shuddered and groaned as he placed a kiss against my temple while breathing heavily. All too soon, his spent cock slipped from my body and I mourned the loss.

"That was fucking amazing," I whispered. "Thank you."

"The jealousy was kinda a turn on," Jake admitted. "And

watching was definitely hot. But the *just us* part was the best."

I smiled and swiped at a tear. "Totally."

"Would you want to do it again? Like a once a year type thing?" Jake asked.

I thought about it for a moment. "Maybe—but no, probably not. Honestly, as long as I have you in my bed, in my life, in my heart? I'm perfectly happy and content—I don't *need* that again. The whole scene was hot, don't get me wrong. But the reason it meant so much was because you love me enough to give me something that makes me happy even if you don't completely understand it. I'll never need anything more than your love and protection."

Jake spent the rest of our *date night* feeding me, plying me with wine and dessert, making love to me, and showing me that I'd never be without his love and protection.

By the time we returned to our pups, we had plenty of stories that Jake swore we'd *never* tell Doc and a lifetime of love to savor and explore.

ALSO BY A.D. ELLIS

Buried Secrets Romantic suspense stand-alone title

Silver in the City (3 books- meet the Silver crew you read about in Forged in the City) Available on AUDIO!

Forged in the City (3 books- a spin-off series from Silver in the City) Available on AUDIO

The BJ Boys Series (3 books, small town, big love) Available on AUDIO

Forever Better Together (friends to lovers) Coming soon to AUDIO!

His Reluctant Cowboy (age gap, opposites attract, cowboy romance) Available on AUDIO!

What Blooms Beneath (LGBT Fantasy romance) Available on AUDIO!

Sawyer

(this was the first M/M I wrote and you may remember Sawyer and Luke being mentioned in Barrett & Ivan as well as in Ryker & Gavin)

Start Something About Him with a **FREE** short story:

(The Beginning https://instafreebie.com/free/84Cxr)

Then continue with the other stand-alone titles in the series (available to read FREE for Kindle Unlimited subscribers):

Bryan & Jase

Brody & Nick

Barrett & Ivan

Braeton & Drew

Ryker & Gavin

Kade & Cameron

Or grab the boxset HERE.

Plus several other titles:

Devoted (a Something About Him novella)

Saving Us

Stranded Hearts (a short story)

Eli & Gage (a Something About Him short story)

A.D.'s first stories (all male/female except Sawyer which is male/male) are in the Torey Hope and Torey Hope: The Later Years series. Find the 8 book box set HERE or you can find each individual title on Amazon.

For Nicky

Because of Beckett

Christmas in Torey Hope

Loving Josie

Decker

Sawyer

Zach

Kendrick

ACKNOWLEDGMENTS

It's always so hard to write this part because I'm worried I'll forget someone without meaning to.

Readers- you are the reason I write. As long as you continue reading my stories, I'll continue writing them. Thank you for your support.

Bloggers- your support, reviews, and promotion are very much appreciated. Thank you!

My author buddies- I don't know that I could keep doing this without our brainstorm sessions, laughter, road trips, meals, wine, and friendship as my support.

Thank you to my alpha readers, betas, editors, proofreaders, and ARC readers! Your eyes and input are beyond important to me.

Brett and Gage- as usual, I doubt you even grasp how much your support, input, and friendship mean to me. This author journey has brought many wonderful things into my life, and you both are two of the BEST! I'm blessed to call you friends.

My family and friends- thank you for your love and support, always.

ABOUT THE AUTHOR

A.D. Ellis is an Indiana girl, born and raised. She spends much of her time in central Indiana as an instructional coach/teacher in the inner city of Indianapolis, being a mom to two amazing school-aged children, and wondering how she and her husband of almost two decades have managed to not drive each other insane. A lot of her time is also devoted to phone call avoidance and her hatred of cooking.

She loves chocolate, wine, pizza, and naps along with reading and writing romance. These loves don't leave much time for housework, much to the chagrin of her husband. Who would pick cleaning the house over a nap or a good book? She uses any extra time to increase her fluency in sarcasm.

Find all of Ellis' contemporary romance and male/male romance at www.adellisauthor.com

FREE books-- sign up at bit.ly/ADEllisNews for a FREE male/female romance.

Sign up at http://www.subscribepage.com/ADEllisNewsMMRomance for a FREE male/male romance book.

www.ingramcontent.com/pod-product-compliance
Lightning Source LLC
Chambersburg PA
CBHW030125260626
47156CB00008B/2803